Praise for

"If George Romero ever (
The Road Warrior, he'd prol.
Eric S. Brown's *The Weaponer*."
> - Peter Clines, author of *Ex-Heroes*

"*The Weaponer* combines the old west with modern technology and an army of the living dead to create a bleak and chilling tale of a post-apocalyptic future. But at its heart, it's a story about the human will to survive."
> - S.G. Browne, author of Breathers

"*The Weaponer* takes the reader into the remnants of the modern world, where old west values take the place of modern comfort in a land of human savages and the zombie curse. Eric S. Brown sculpts his story, like The Weaponer, as 'an artisan of death.'"
> - Bowie V. Ibarra, author of the *Down the Road* series

"With *The Weaponer*, Eric S. Brown reloads the zombie genre for a take-no-prisoners tale of action, heartbreak and adventure."
> - Jonathan Maberry,
> *New York Times* bestselling author
> of *Patient Zero* and *Dead of Night*

Also by Eric S. Brown

Space Stations and Graveyards
Dying Days
Portals of Terror
Madmen's Dreams
Cobble
The Queen
The Wave
Waking Nightmares
Zombies II: Inhuman
Unabridged Unabashed and Undead
The War of the Worlds Plus Blood, Guts
and Zombies (with H.G. Wells)
Season of Rot
Barren Earth (with Stephen North)
World War of the Dead
How the West Went to Hell
Bigfoot War
Antiheroes (with David Dunwoody)
Martin Kier and the Dead
The Human Experiment

COSCOM ENTERTAINMENT MONSTER NOVELLA SERIES

The Weaponer

Eric S. Brown

Introduction by Joe McKinney

COSCOM ENTERTAINMENT
WINNIPEG

ISBN 978-1-926712-70-3

PUBLISHED BY COSCOM ENTERTAINMENT
www.coscomentertainment.com
Text set in Garamond; Printed and bound in the USA
COVER ART BY GARY MCCLUSKEY
COVER DESIGN BY COSCOM ENTERTAINMENT

This book is dedicated to my family and my fans
in thanks for their constant support.

AN INTRODUCTION TO ERIC S. BROWN'S
THE WEAPONER

by Joe McKinney

Horror plays nice with others.

Other genres, I mean.

Look at horror and romance. Natural bedfellows. How about horror and the coming of age story? Old friends. Horror and science fiction? Anybody seen that movie Alien? How about *A Clockwork Orange*? What about horror and crime fiction? Again, no problem. After all, what is a ghost story but a scary cold case?

So, really, it shouldn't be any surprise at all that the horror story and the western fit together as well as they do. Past masters, like Robert E. Howard, and present day pros like Joe R. Lansdale, have even turned the marriage of the frontier and the terrifying into an art form as authentically unique as the blues.

But how is it that the horror story and the western can come together to form more than the sum of their parts? The western story, after all, is the ultimate expression of Realism. Great Realist writers like Emile Zola and Frank Norris would have been proud, I think, to see the careful attention western writers like Elmore Leonard and Zane Grey and Louis L'Amour paid to the minutia of frontier life. But horror, on the other hand, deals entirely with the intrusion of the extraordinary into the ordinary, thereby denying Realism on the most fundamental level. At first blush, the two genres would seem to be mutually exclusive.

And yet they are not.

I think we sense this kinship between the two genres

more than we intellectualize it. But veteran writers, like the ones I've already mentioned, and up and coming stars like Eric S. Brown, have shown that the bond between the horror story and the western is compelling enough to bear closer examination.

So what is the weird alchemy that makes them function so well together?

The obvious common ground is violence. Life on the frontier was short and brutal, the future always uncertain. Horror presents its characters with the same grim possibilities. Whether our hero is stalked by a pack of werewolves, hunted down by vampires, or surrounded by zombies, death comes hard and fast, and the future is little more than a cruel joke.

But I suspect that the violence is only a symptom of the mechanism, and not the mechanism itself. The deeper connection, the real reason the hybrid love child of the horror story and the western is such a beautiful baby, is because both genres ultimately are attempts to test the fragility of man against the rock of the world. Whether the enemy is a band of bank robbers on the run, an enraged war party of Apache, the demon Pazuzu, or Bob Gray, a.k.a. Pennywise the Clown, is ultimately incidental to the real struggle, which is proving once and for all that a man's life has value, even in its transience.

Eric S. Brown understands that. And the book you're holding in your hands right now is proof of how thoroughly he's plumbed this issue.

It rained here last night. As the storm came in I went out to the back patio with a cold beer and a manuscript copy of this book, and read it to the rhythm of the rain hitting my roof. More than once I stopped reading and stared out at the rain, struck by how perfectly Eric S. Brown captured the essence of both the western and the horror tale, how seamlessly he worked in the fundamental question common to both genres:

How much is a man's life worth?

To his credit, Eric S. Brown answers this question by pushing beyond the conventions of both the horror story and the western.

And in the process, shows us a man discovering his world anew.

Don't get me wrong. Like any great western, or survival horror story for that matter, this is a violent tale. There are zombies and cannibals here, after all. But the real meat of this story is not in its bite, but in its yearning to explore the world in which it's set. A post-apocalyptic frontier peopled by the sick and the deranged and the insatiable dead is all around Alan, the Weaponer. But so too is this idea of the wall that surrounds the world.

And that wall is, I think, Eric S. Brown's stroke of genius.

To ponder its existence is human. But to go beyond it is to enter mythic space. That is a hero's job. It is like Ulysses entering the world of the dead. Alan the Weaponer is the prototypical western hero, a common man displaying uncommon courage, and in using such a man to fill the role of epic hero, Eric S. Brown has given us something new, something special.

This is where the western and the horror story come together. Alan the Weaponer must decide exactly what his life is worth. And he must fight for what's right with his courage and his skill, and also with his humanity. He has nothing to fall back on but himself.

It is the same inner struggle faced by Will Kane, the marshal played by Gary Cooper in the film *High Noon*.

And also by Father Karras in *The Exorcist*.

What is the cost of courage, and what is the price of cowardice?

Well, Eric S. Brown has the answer for you, and so I'll leave you in his capable hands.

Go ahead and turn the page. I think you'll find he has a few surprises for you.

November 22, 2010
San Antonio, TX

The Weaponer

Eric S. Brown

Introduction by Joe McKinney

PROLOGUE

LONG AGO, IN the last days of the fall of man, Colonel Hannes Verne stood on top of the hastily constructed, cobbled together wall of concrete and brick , watching as the final convoy of buses and supply trucks drove towards the gates. Verne knew his own supply of mortars, grenades, and the like was nearly exhausted. The dead were pressed hundreds deep against the wall and unless he could come up with a plan to disperse the ones at the gates, opening it would be suicide.

Verne rubbed his hands together to warm them in the chill of the morning air. The fate of the people in the approaching convoy rested solely with him and his men. Those civilians were counting on him to save their lives and get them inside.

The wall stood thirty feet tall and at many places along its length Verne's men were occupied with the fight to hold back the dead so its construction could be completed. He was reluctant to expend any of his dwindling firepower. There were already over a thousand civilians inside and sheltered at the makeshift town that was being set up many miles from where he stood. He wasn't up to making a call like this one, deciding who lived and who died. All the generals were dead and rotting, and like it or not he was the highest ranking officer left in the United States military.

His men had one advantage over the civilians: each of them were injected with a vaccine that allowed them to stand against the dead without the worry of a simple bite or scratch turning them into one of the monsters below.

The vaccine was costly and difficult to produce; there would never be any more of it.

It was against orders for him to draft help from the town to defend the wall. The advantage given to them by the vaccine was a true blessing, but it didn't make his men invincible. The dead could still rip them to pieces as easy as they could anyone else. Verne shook his head and knew he didn't have the manpower or firepower left to open the gates this time if he wanted to preserve what was already being built inside the wall's perimeter.

He tapped on his comlink. "Keep the gates closed. If they try to ram their way in, take them out hard and fast."

Colonel Verne headed for the stairs leading down to the bunker below to oversee the next batch of dead that was being let in through the specimen gates for Dr. Watkins to study. The order he'd just given was the hardest of his career and he didn't want to be around to see it carried through. Helping Dr. Watkins was as good of an excuse as any to get away as gunfire tore through the early morning air.

1

THE SUN PEEKED over the distant hills, spilling in through the window. A rooster crowed as Alan sat up in bed. The morning air was touched by a crisp chill. There was a lot of work to be done today if he had the time to do it. Rumors were flying *they* were inside now. Alan didn't believe the stories, but he believed in the power of fear. It could make even the best men do questionable things. With a yawn and stretch, he plopped his bare feet onto the cold wood of the floor. He threw on his clothes without pausing to glance in the mirror. The boys would be here soon and this time they'd want more than his normal handiwork. They'd be needing him and the cannon.

Alan noticed the fire had died down during the night so he stoked it back to life. He lingered by the warmth of the stove, banishing the chill of sleep from his body. There was some coffee left in the pot from the night before sitting on top of the stove. Pouring himself a cup, he took a sip of its bitter blackness. Coffee was a rare thing, but his job in Hyattsburg had its perks. He'd convinced the boys he couldn't work without it so he always had some on hand. Alan was very thankful for Doc West. Without the old man's green houses and his strange talent to grow almost anything, there might not have been any coffee at all. His own family didn't have the title of "doctor" like the Wests, the Camerons, and the Gorios, but he and his dad were still considered among the elite of the town. The Wests were crazy. The Gorios were known for their charity and were the only real healers of the bunch. The Camerons caused folks to wonder how they'd ever gotten the title of doctor for their family. The Gorios' estate riddled with odd contraptions, plastic boxes with flat sheets of glass on their fronts like mirrors, and junk that seemed to serve no purpose yet had been passed down even if the knowledge meant to accompany them hadn't fully been. The family continued to fall from grace with each passing season. Debt weighed heavily on them and there didn't seem to be any relief for them in sight. They were terrible farmers and none of them good, strong men. Alan thanked God his dad had passed down not only his knowledge to him correctly, but taught him to be a man as well.

The sound of approaching horses told Alan that Zek and the boys had arrived. He shrugged on his coat and fastened his gun belt around his waist, then headed out to meet them. Alan stood on his porch as they rode in. Zek, of course, was in the lead, with Wike and Mathew at his side. Alan counted a dozen other riders with them.

He nodded at Zek as the lawman hopped to the dirt and walked towards him.

"Mornin'. Reckon' I don't have to ask what brings you by."

"Mornin', Alan," he said. "So I gather you heard, then?"

"Yep." Alan nodded. "Good old Doctor West dropped in on me last night. Old fella was a more than a mite worked up. *They* really coming?"

"Don't know for sure. Could have been coyotes that got the Byrnes. Some kind of animal, maybe. Doc Gorio swears otherwise, but I don't rightly see how it could be them things. Heck, we ain't had a problem with 'em since I was born here in Hyattsburg other than the occasional screw up with our own." Zek tugged at his hat and then got out his case to roll up a smoke. "We gotta check it out though. Can't take no chances when it comes to something like this. Gonna need likely everything you got and then some."

"And then some?" Alan asked, knowing what was coming next.

"Sorry, I know killin' ain't what you do for a living, but we're gonna need your skills and know-how out there with us . . ." Zek paused. "We're gonna need it, too, Alan . . . the cannon."

"Can't say I am happy to hear that, but I figured you'd be askin'. I got her ready last night after Doc left. How much ammo you boys carrying?"

"None of us got more than a handful of rounds apiece except Wike there."

"There's plenty in the depot outback. Got enough maybe for, I'd say, a couple of hundred rounds each. That's gonna have to be enough. Got no time to make more if you're gonna drag me out there with ya'll."

"It'll do." Zek smiled, seemingly thankful. "You always were a dependable man, Alan." To Wike and Mathew: "Boys, go get that ammo loaded up. Make sure to divide it up evenly, now. We're all gonna be watching each other's backs out there in the sand."

"You need guns, too?" Alan asked reluctantly.

"Some of the boys here got stuff that belonged to their grandpas. You sure know we do, if you got something better we can use."

Alan sighed. "There's a new cache of rifles I just got done with not too long back, five of them. Take those if you want, but don't touch my other stuff."

"You heard the man!" Zek yelled at his deputies. "Don't touch nothin' 'less he says it's all right."

Alan nodded in thanks. "The cannon ain't exactly easy to carry on a horse, Zek."

"Wike'll help you get it loaded up. No fear of that."

"Come on, Doc," Wike said to Alan. "Let's get to it."

Alan shot him a look. "I ain't no doctor."

"Could've fooled me." Wike laughed. "You know things the rest of us couldn't figure if we had a lifetime to try."

Alan shrugged. "Still don't make me a doctor. Besides, being smart ain't everything."

Wike followed Alan around the house. Alan led him to the workshop beside the depot where the others were stuffing their packs full of rounds for their rifles and pistols. His forge sat cold and locked up in the distance. He opened the heavy door and heard Wike take a sharp breath as it creaked open and the man got a look inside. The walls were covered nearly from floor to ceiling with every type of gun one could imagine. There were a few even Alan himself didn't have a full handle on yet. Stacks of bullets and rounds in numerous shapes and sizes lay about in cluttered stacks and piles. Molds, hammers and other tools of Alan's trade filled the bulk of the room and were in pristine condition. It was clear to anyone Alan loved his work and took a great deal of pride in it.

Wike stopped and stood staring at a strange-looking rifle on the wall. Its tag read "AK-47."

Alan smiled. "They sure don't make them like that anymore."

Wike chuckled. "You're the only one who makes them at all, Alan."

"Couldn't build one of those if I wanted. That's why I stick to simpler ones for you and the other men. None of you seem to complain."

"Hades no! Your guns are works of art. I had one passed on to me from my pa, but it jammed about every third shot. Ain't never seen one of yours do that."

"You're overly kind, but I do hope my handiwork does its job."

"You can count on that," Wike said.

Alan headed to the rear of the workshop and lifted the heavy tarp that covered his father's cannon. He didn't know how his father had gotten it. Likely, he'd traded some old man out of it for a fraction of what it was really worth. Of course, without his dad's know-how to get it fixed up and running, it was worthless. Alan'd taken great care of it since his dad had passed. He'd never had the occasion to fire it, but he'd seen his dad do it as a lad and was taught all about how to maintain it and its belt-feeding mechanism.

Wike whistled. "Now that's a gun. How many barrels does that thing have?"

"Enough," Alan said. "Zek and the others are waiting. We best get to it."

Lugging the thing around was a chore, though it was designed where one man could fire it effectively assuming he was strong enough. Wike helped Alan get it out of the workshop and strapped onto a horse. Zek had brought an extra one just for him. There were also three horses without riders that looked to be loaded with supplies and now also carried some of the ammo Zek's boys had gathered from Alan's stockpile.

Alan didn't own a horse. Never saw the need for one. After his dad had passed on, he kept pretty much to himself and his work. He had no wife and wasn't familiar with any prospects that struck his liking. It often troubled him that his father's line would likely end with him, but there was little he could do about it. Hyattsburg kept him busy with the demand for ammo and gun repair. He even took on custom jobs from time to time if the pay was good enough. He was far from hurting for money, not that he ever used it. Alan generally just traded for anything he needed or got it as part of his family's longstanding deal with Hyattsburg's lawmen and governing body.

Alan looked over the horse Zek had brought for him. It was massive, black, and well-muscled. It was the best looking horse in the whole posse other than Zek's.

"You ready?" Zek called to him.

"Just a few more things," Alan said and darted back into his house to make sure everything was locked up tight and safe. He grabbed the last gift his father had given him off the mantle and shoved it in his pocket. Spotting his coffee still on the stove, he took another hit of it then ventured back out to face the day.

The posse rode out, leaving Alan's estate in the dust behind them. He looked back at his house, his workshops, forges, and the ammo depot. His family had been so blessed. Only the three doctors of Hyattsburg had homes as large and vast as his own. He wondered what would become of it if he didn't make it back since he had no heir. He decided he'd rather not know. Most likely, the council would have it looted for everything remotely useful to the town because without him, weapons would become short in supply very quickly if the creatures had found a way inside.

The posse rode hard towards the Byrnes' farm. It was as good a place as any to start in their search and Alan figured Zek hoped Wike might be able to tell more about what he and Dr. Gorio had there.

Wike was the best tracker in the whole town. The weather had been clear and there was at least a small chance he would be able to find a trail.

As the men slowed their horses and crossed onto Byrne's land, Zek turned to Alan. "When I came yesterday and found the bodies, I was alone. Hadn't seen John at the saloon the night before. He's always there stirring up something. Usually drunker than a skunk. Had to lock him up more than once this year. Him not being there was peculiar. I decided I would ride out and see if the family was doing all right. I knew his boy, Clint, had the lung disease. Thought they might be in need. About lost my lunch when I saw little Clint torn up like he was. I hightailed it back to town for the Doc and some extra guns. Didn't know of any in the area from the folks in town and ain't never seen a wild one that didn't travel in a pack. If there was more than one, I wasn't about to face them on my own with a single pistol that had less than six rounds in my holster."

"So you came back after that?" Alan asked.

"Sure did. I brought five men and Dr. Gorio. Couldn't find Wike at the time, though. He was off on one of his hunts. We checked the area, but didn't find anything. Dr. Gorio took one look at the bodies and started telling us it was *them*, though. Look, Alan, if we do have them things running loose, they gotta be dealt with fast before they stumble onto someone else like the Byrnes. They were good folks and surely didn't deserve what they got. If there's a trail to be found here, don't you worry none, Wike will find it. Got some Indian blood in him, that boy does. Could find a needle in a haystack if he knew it went in there."

The company came to a halt. Zek and Alan stayed in their saddles talking, while Wike and a few of the others were already taking a look around for the trail Zek hoped for. The others in the party dismounted and headed across the lawn to check out the house and the barn. Sometimes the creatures were smart. They would hide indoors during the hours the sun filled the sky and lay in ambush for any poor soul unlucky enough to happen upon them. Mathew, with his Winchester in hand, led the group headed for the barn.

Within a few minutes, everyone gathered again at the

horses with Zek and Alan. The whole place was clean and not even Wike had anything to show for his efforts. If there had been a trail, time and sand had covered it over.

"Well, boys, maybe there's nothing to this after all. Doc Gorio has been wrong before," Zek said, and Alan hoped very much the lawman was right.

"Just 'cause there ain't no trail now doesn't mean they weren't here," Wike said. "We still don't really know anything more than we did. Long time has passed since you was first here, Zek. Could be the things hit the Byrnes, had their meal, and hightailed it back into the desert."

Alan's hope sank at hearing this. It meant he wasn't off the hook yet.

"You could be right," Zek said. "Don't like leaving the town with so many of us gone, but I reckon we should split up and ride into the sand some to be sure."

"The desert is a mighty big place, Zek," Mathew said. "No one I know of has crossed it since Hyattsburg was founded."

"He's right," Alan added. "The odds of us finding anything just riding around out there are next to nothing."

"What's the matter, you yellow, Doc?" Wike said.

"I ain't no 'doc,'" Alan told him again. "I ain't yellow either. Just saying what we all know is true. We could ride for days, scour a mile in every direction, and still find nothing."

"You're right," Wike said, "but you're forgetting one thing: they might find us."

"Oh, I would say you can count on that if they're out there. The smell of live flesh will bring them running," Mathew said.

"Well, I for one would rather go looking than sit at home and wait on them to come to me if they are out there," Zek said. "All we need to do is find some small sign of them and Wike can take it from there and we'll know where we stand. Sorry, Alan, but Wike's right. We need to try." Zek nodded at one of the youngest riders with them, a green boy named Bill. "Lad, you head on back to town. Let folks know what we're doing and get them ready in case those things do come a callin' while we're gone."

"Yes, sir," Bill replied. He rode off hard and fast for Hyattsburg as Alan jealously stared after him.

"Maybe we should stop at the Camerons?" a man Alan thought went by the name of David said. "The family used to talk to the sky-eyes. Maybe they still can. It'll spare us a lot of legwork."

Zek shook his head as most of the other men laughed and snorted. "The Camerons are the most useless, good-for-nothing excuses for doctors who ever lived."

Wike said, "If there ever was such a crazy thing as eyes in the sky, there sure ain't now. The Camerons will be a waste of time."

David turned red and kept quiet as Zek took the others' attention off of him. "Listen up now. There's fifteen of us. We'll break up into three groups of five and each take a different direction. We'll ride out for the rest of today, go a bit farther tomorrow when we're fresh in the morning, then head back. We'll all meet up right here in about a day and a half. I'll lead the group heading west. Wike, Mathew, pick your men and take the east and the north. Alan, you're with Wike." Zek gave them all a hard look. "Well, what you waiting on? Let's get to it, boys!"

2

WIKE, ALAN, LOUIS, Robert, and Ed rode hard. The midday sun was hot and blistering as they left the Byrne farmstead behind them and headed out into the sands. Wike was in the lead. They brought one of the supply horses and Louis led it along with them. The group moved slower for it, but there was nothing to be done about that. Alan wasn't used to this kind of exposure. He unscrewed his canteen and took a mouthful of water.

Robert, a burly and unshaved man with leather-like skin, rode up next to him. "Go easy on that. Ain't exactly a lot of places out here to get it filled up again."

Everyone seemed tense and on edge, like they were riding through the calm before the storm. Alan wondered if any of even these hardened men were really ready to face the creatures. He himself hadn't seen one since he was a child. The experience sometimes still found him in his nightmares. When he was ten, there had been an escape in Hyattsburg. Mr. Green's daughter, Diana, had passed away from pneumonia. No one ever found out exactly what happened, but folks guessed old Mr. Green didn't have the heart to put her down. He was found the next day with his jaw gnawed off and most of the flesh sucked off the bones from his thick legs. An alarm went up right away and just like today, a posse was formed and sent out to find her. The things were often very slow unless they had their prey in sight. They'd just wander around seemingly without direction until they caught the smell of flesh. The posse then wasn't able to find Diana in time. She made her way to Alan's home. His dad had been out working in the forge, trying to figure out how to make smaller parts for the weapons he was building. Alan sat in the kitchen at the table, beaming as his mother cooked. The smell of eggs and freshly baked bread were in the air when a knock sounded on the door. There was something odd about it. It sounded off somehow as the blow on the door seemed to have been awkwardly struck. Alan watched as his mother moved to open the door and stared in horror at the blood-soaked little girl that waited there. His mother never had time to scream.

Diana hurled herself at her like a cougar, all teeth and nails. Alan cried out in fear and leaped to his feet as his mom went down under the girl. Blood sprayed from the hole Diana's teeth ripped in his mother's throat. Her face was a mess from the girl's constant clawing from the struggled. Not knowing what else to do and unable to get by the two of them to go after his dad, Alan dug out his pocket knife. He moved in and plunged it into Diana. The blade slid easily into the dead girl's neck and cut it open, leaving a long, deep gash across her throat. A black, syrup-like fluid ran from the wound. The girl paid him no attention though. If she'd felt his attack at all, she didn't show it. She continued her assault on his mother. The entire floor was covered with blood and Alan slipped in it as he tried to back away. He fell hard, his head striking the edge of the table; darkness took him. Many hours later, when he came to, he was clean and in his bed. His father sat in the corner of his room, watching him from a chair with sad eyes and a distant gaze. He knew in that moment his mother was gone. He'd never seen his dad cry before, but as they stared at each other in silence, Alan believed he saw a tear roll from his father's cheeks.

The memory was seared on his heart, a painful

reminder of what the dead could do to a person.

Alan shifted in his saddle. The day's search was long and when night finally came, Alan was ready to be on his feet for a while. Wike was disappointed at their lack of success in finding anything useful and looked to blame himself. The tracker plopped onto the ground and let the others do the work of making camp for the night. They built a small fire, passed some jerky around, and a pot of coffee was put on. Alan took a seat by the fire as Louis attended to the coffee. Robert made sure the horses were tended to while Ed took first watch standing somewhere out in the sands beyond the light of the fire with his rifle ready in case the dead came calling.

"Don't get upset, Wike," Louis said. "It's tough country out here and time is against us. There just wasn't a trail to find."

Robert joined them at the fire. "Louis is right. If they're out here, I expect we'll see them tonight."

Alan drew his pistol from his holster and began to take it apart to clean it.

"What kind of gun is that?" Wike asked, seeming to come out of his funk. "Ain't never seen one like it before."

"It's called a Glock," Alan said. "It was my grandfather's. My dad passed it on to me when he died."

"Looks like a tough gun," Wike said admiringly.

"It is," Alan said, nodding. "9mm rounds, 17-round clip. It was built to take wear and keep on shooting."

"Ain't nothing like what you build for us," Robert said.

Alan couldn't tell if the man was jealous or not. "There are a lot of weapons from the old world that just can't be made anymore. I don't know how to make plastics like they used to. Dad taught me all about metal and such, though. The six-guns I make for Hyattsburg are tough in their own right. They may not have the Glock's high capacity clip or its rate of fire, but they work and their ammo is relatively easy to make. Never had a complaint before."

"You better shut your mouth now, Robert," Wike growled. "Ain't the gun that matters anyway; it's the man using it. Ain't that right, Alan?"

Louis chuckled at the exchange. "I for one am thankful Hyattsburg has you, Alan. Your dad was a heck of a man. Always did what was right and was fair in his dealings. It was a real shame what happened to him and your mom. Don't think he ever made peace with what happened to her."

"Wasn't his fault," Alan said quietly. "I think it killed him in the end more than the sickness. He held on for years, for my sake, but he was never the same. His smile was broken."

"What about you, Alan?" Wike asked. "What are we gonna do when you're gone? Don't matter how much you got stored up, it won't last long enough."

"You need a wife. Get a boy so you get him learned up on all the stuff you know like them doctors teach their kids," Louis said, reaching for the coffee. He poured a cup and handed it to him.

Alan took it, thankful. His throat was dry and the sun hadn't been kind to him.

"He ain't gonna get no wife," Robert said. The others turned to look at him. "Well, it's the truth. Now, I ain't known you long, Alan, but I can already see you're a man who don't like people. Don't know if you're bitter or it's just your way, but unless you change, ain't no woman in her right mind shackin' up with you."

Alan wondered if he should feel angry at Robert's remark, but he didn't. He wondered if his dad would have leapt up with fire in his eyes and knocked Robert off his cocky bottom into the dirt. Instead, he just shrugged. "Got my work. That's all I need."

"That may be true, but Hyattsburg needs more from you," Wike said.

"Then why am I here risking my life to chase down these things if I am so important?" Alan said. This he did get angry at.

Wike didn't have an answer it seemed, so stayed silent.

Louis took control and changed the subject. "I got next watch with Robert. You should get some sleep while you can, Alan."

3

THE NIGHT GREW darker and the camp fell silent as Louis and Robert relieved Ed of his watch. Wike never headed for his bedroll. The man moved closer to the fire, drawing a massive knife from his belt and went to work on sharpening its blade. Alan took Louis's wisdom to heart and stretched out on his bedroll. Sleeping on the ground wasn't as bad as he thought it would be. It reminded him of camping with his dad as a child. He lay on his back looking up at the stars. They were bright tonight and the sky was filled with them. The cannon had been unloaded and lay next him. He'd prepped it and gotten it ready just in case, but he hoped in his heart the dead wouldn't come. He wasn't filled with a sense of vengeance directed at them like some would've been. He wasn't even scared exactly. Alan wanted to go home, plain and simple. This wasn't his place or his job. They very well could run the cannon without him and if it broke down, it wasn't like he was going to be able to fix it in the middle of a firefight without a miracle.

He sighed and let his tired eyes close. His sleep wasn't a restful one. Instead it was more like his mind repeatedly worked things over.

Alan didn't want to believe the things were inside the wall with them. In fact, he didn't see how it was possible. Most of Hyattsburg's citizens knew very little about the wall. Some even thought it was a myth or a story made up just to keep people from traveling over the desert. No one had rode to it and returned since long before he'd been born. But wall or not, the dead had stayed out of

Hyattsburg. If they were out there en mass as every one of the legends claimed, something certainly kept them away. Alan's father had known more than most about such things. His great grandfather had passed down the story of the fall and the flight, and though it couldn't entirely be taken as literal truth today, Alan knew his father had put a good bit of stock in it. He'd said, "There's some truth in every story. You just need to know how to find it."

The story went that long ago the world of man was a very different place. The whole world belonged to man. People had lived everywhere, so his father told him. There were even some who lived in houses made of metal and plastic that floated among the very stars of the skies above. Man had everything. There were places called hospitals that worked wonders in healing the sick and sometimes even saved the dying. There were "copters" that flew through the air on whirling blades and danced like humming birds. The roads that now lay crumpled and littered with the dead husks of vehicles from the old world were alive then, traveled on by such wondrous things as "cars" and "trucks." These "cars" could go faster and farther than any horse. They had such things as "air conditioning" and "shocks" that allowed the rider to travel in comfort over more miles in a day than a horse could travel in several. And the weapons . . . Alan's dad told him of marvels that even now made him believe his father had been exaggerating. His dad said there were bombs that could level entire cities many times the size of Hyattsburg, and others that could destroy hundreds of miles or more with their "fallout," whatever that was. There were also things called Bio-weapons. His father also spoke of these as if their very name was a swear word and often spat into the dirt when he mentioned them.

They had no honor, he said. They were weapons that killed randomly without direction or discretion. He said some believed this type of weapon might have even given birth to the dead.

In the old world of man, the dead had stayed dead. It wasn't until something had happened and the dead began to rise that the world fell. No one really knew what started it, but no one—not even the great "military" his grandfather had spoken so strongly of—could stop them. The creatures awoke hungry and took what they thought was theirs. Sadly, that included every living man, woman and child on the planet. The human race fought hard, but in the end the dead's numbers simply grew too quickly. Even the use of the nightmarish bombs his great grandfather had told tales of couldn't stop them. The radiation didn't affect them; all it did was hurt the earth itself, so those kinds of bombs were only used at the end in times of the greatest desperation.

This land they lived in that once was called the "United States" gave up its land to the dead, miles and miles every day as resources and manpower for the war continued to shrink. The wall was supposedly built as a last-ditch effort to ensure that some would survive the dead's onslaught. It was one of the greatest achievements of the old world, considering how quickly it was assembled given its size. The best and the brightest left of those in the old world were admitted behind it first along with the remainder of the military. In the end, though, anyone still breathing was allowed to gain entrance behind the wall. Its construction was completed, numerous battles fought atop it, then something happened . . . . Not even his great grandfather had known what, but no one heard from the wall again. Parties were sent out from the newly born city of Hyattsburg to check on it, but none returned. Life went on and things changed over time.

The number of those left alive shrunk as well. The city became a town, knowledge grew rarer, talents were lost to death, illness, and the dead. Controlling their own dead and dealing with them were a top priority in an effort to keep Hyattsburg alive though. It may not be the wonder it was in the stories, but all of its residents were proud of what it had become. It was place of good folks. There were few malcontents in its populace and people looked after each other. Everyone did their share and for the most part folks were happy.

The paradox lay in that if the wall was real, how could have the dead suddenly gotten inside after all these years? Because if the wall wasn't real, what had kept the dead away from Hyattsburg for so long?

Alan kept rolling it over in his mind, but he knew without more information, there simply was no way to know the real truth of things.

ꝯ

FAR TO THE west, under the same stars, Zek sat watch with a man named Crawford while the others of their party slept. The meager fire of their encampment crackled and a slight breeze caused its embers to flit about on the wind as Zek stared into its blaze.

"That Alan boy is a mite odd, Zek. You sure he's gonna be able to handle himself if Wike runs into trouble?"

Zek looked at Crawford. "His dad was a good man. I think he will be, too, given time."

Something moved in the shadows beyond the light of the fire. "What was that?" Crawford asked.

Zek drew his six shooter as Crawford chambered a round in his rifle. The lawman strained his eyes, squinting into the darkness. Something flew at them from the shadows. Zek turned to see Crawford clutching at a metal shaft that protruded from his chest. A stain of red grew under his hands as he struggled to rip it out. Another arrow flew into the camp, striking Crawford again. This second arrow sunk deeper into Crawford than the first, puncturing a lung with a sick kind of wet popping noise as it wedged itself between his ribs. Blood leaked from his mouth as he gave Zek a final look and toppled over onto the sand.

Zek opened fire. His hand flew as he pumped three shots in the direction the arrow had come from. "Up!" he wailed. "Everybody up! We're under attack!"

Ronnie rolled up from his bedroll with both his six shooters blazing in the same direction Zek fired.

Don moved slower, bringing his shotgun to bare on

the spot, but held his fire. "What are we shooting at?"

"Don't know," Zek shouted. "Something out there just killed Crawford."

The night had grown quiet again around them. Zek eyed the edge of the camp. "We need to find some cover."

"Uh, Zek," Ronnie said. "The horses are gone."

"Dang it."

"Smitty is dead, too," Don added.

Zek walked carefully over to where the other had been sleeping. An arrow like the one that killed Crawford stuck up through Smitty's bedroll. A pool of blood seeped into the sand around the man's body.

"What the devil's going on?" Don said. "Are we fighting Indians, here?"

Zek resisted the urge to smash the butt of his six gun into the back of Don's skull. "You idiot. This ain't the old west. There's no Indians out here. It's just us and the dead."

"Ain't never seen a dead man who could use a bow," Ronnie said.

"You ever seen a walking dead man, Ronnie?" Zek snarled. Ronnie shook his head. "Then keep your mouth shut. I'm trying to think, here."

Several more whistling noises slashed through the air towards them.

"Down!" Zek shouted before an arrow caught him in the back. It slammed into Zek's spine and he knew he was a goner before he hit the sand. There'd be no getting it out without killing him for sure. Zek saw Ronnie go down, too. Three arrows tore into him from various angles and crisscrossed in his chest. Don's shotgun thundered then fell silent. Zek's soiled shirt and homespun jeans became stained and grew warm from the flow of his own blood as it ran from his flesh. He tried to roll over and failed. The attempt sent waves of hellish pain through his body as tears welled up in his eyes. Zek fought them down, gritting his teeth and made sure he still held onto his pistol. He was determined to stay alive long enough to see the man that was his murderer. It was a decision he quickly came to regret as a group of wild, feral men came charging at him with their blades waving above their heads. Zek shot the man in the lead; the man fell from a simple stomach wound, howling in pain. It was too dark to see the man clearly, but Zek knew the man couldn't be dead if he felt pain. Then wild men came for Zek. Their knives and hatchets rose and fell in a righteous rhythm of fury. A dagger poked its way into his arm as an ax blade took off one of Zek's ears and part of his scalp. He moaned, barely conscious. Zek weakly lifted his six gun for another shot but never got the chance. A massive man dressed in rags and animal skins filled his field of vision and smashed a hatchet deep into his skull.

5

ALAN AWOKE WITH Wike's boot prodding him. "Time to ride, sleepyhead," the tracker said.

Alan sat up and realized he missed breakfast. The fire was extinguished and the others were almost ready to get moving. "Sorry," Alan mumbled, wiping the sleep from his eyes. "Any coffee left?"

Wike smiled. "Had a feeling you'd be wanting some. Saved you a cup. It's over there."

Alan got up and tucked away his bedroll. He found the cup Wike left him in the sand by the cold fire and guzzled half of it in a single swallow as soon as he thought it was cool. "You loaded up the cannon?"

Wike nodded. "No time to waste, and you were so peaceful getting your beauty rest."

Alan laughed. "Thanks."

"Taking it apart is a whole lot easier than putting it together."

"Always is." Alan shrugged on his coat and fastened his gun belt around his waist after a quick check of his Glock.

"Hope Zek and the others are having better luck at finding something out here than we are," Wike said as he swung into his saddle. "I got a feeling today's going to be just as big of a waste as yesterday."

"Hope you're right," Alan said with a smile, climbing onto his horse.

"Lousy attitude."

Alan knew it was, but all he still wanted was to just go home.

With a shout, Wike led the group onward, riding hard from the camp. They left a trail of dust in their wake. The group soon slowed so they could look for any sign of the dead in the sand. The plan was to ride out a ways more, try to find a sign of the dead or anything unusual, then hightail it back to the Byrnes's farm and meet up with the others before nightfall. Wike and Alan rode side-by–side, the others following.

"Alan?" Wike asked. "You ever think about heading out to the wall? Ya know, to see if it's real?"

"I wonder about what's out there as much as anyone else, but no. I'm an indoors kind of man. My work keeps me busy enough. It's easy for me to lose myself in seeing what I can save of the old world, while trying to come up with things of my own for the time we live in now."

"But don't you want to know? Seems an awful waste, in a way, for everyone to just stay back and assume the stories are true. Real ignorance, if you ask me."

"Yeah, but I heard an old saying once."

"What's that?"

"Ignorance is bliss."

The day was just as hot as the one before and the sun had yet to reach its zenith in the sky. Alan wiped the sweat on his brow and took a slow, careful sip from his canteen. The water felt like heaven as it ran down his dry throat. As they rode on, he kept an eye on the small hilltops around them as Wike scoured the ground.

"Hey, Wike," Alan called. "What's that?" He pointed to a small, odd shape on top of one of the hills to their left.

Wike took a look, squinting against the rays of the sun. "Can't make it out. Almost looks like some kind of sign or something."

"You think we should check it out?"

The man smiled. "Do you really have to ask?" The

tracker dismounted. "You stay here." He turned to the others. "Stay alert. Ain't never known the dead to post signs, but ya never know."

Wike scurried up the side of the small, rocky hill. It was tough going. It was hard to find handholds in the rock and the sandy gravel was slippery in most spots. As Wike neared the top, Alan pulled an old world pair of binoculars from his pack and raised them to get a better view. He felt sick as he saw what was waiting on Wike at the top. It was a human head, rotting in the heat of the sun, and mounted onto a sharpened stick that was shoved through its skull. Through the binoculars, Wike appeared as if he wanted to yell back and let them know what he'd found, but held his tongue. If whoever did this was still around, and there was no need to give them his exact position if they didn't have it already. Besides, Wike's hold on the rock face was precarious at best and appeared to take he had to pull himself the rest of the way up. As Wike finished his climb and slid onto the top of the hill next to the head, he took it in intently. Alan saw him mouth the words "Oh Lord, have mercy on us," as Mathew's good eye stared back at him. The other was gone, likely picked out by a bird or some animal before they'd arrived.

At last, Wike gave in and vomited. He wretched up his breakfast of jerky and coffee into the circle of congealed blood at the base of the spike. He glanced at the others then appeared to survey the area around them from his new vantage point. He motioned down to Alan the area was clear. Wike wiped the remains of the vomit from his face and lips with the back of his shirt sleeve, then took a breath to steady himself before starting back down the rocky slope.

The second his feet hit the ground, he said, "We got to move now!"

The others looked at Wike with confused and surprised expressions. None of them questioned him, however, and kept their mouths shut. They leapt into their saddles as Wike took his own. Wike kicked the sides of his horse and lit out as fast as its legs would go. It seemed like a good idea to Alan so he followed after him. After a couple of miles, Wike lessened their pace. His skin was pale as if he'd seen a ghost, and his manner suggested he was as frightened as was possible for a man such as him.

"What did you see up there?" Louis asked,, not realizing Alan had seen everything just as well through his binoculars. .

"We need to get back to Hyattsburg," was all Wike said.

"Why?" Louis asked. "What's going on?"

"That was Mathew's head," he said. "Somebody cut it off his shoulders and stuck it up there for us to find. Whoever killed the Byrnes was likely who got Mathew and his boys, too. Don't you see? They're out here with us in the sands, watching us."

"Mathew's head?" Ed said.

"We're not hunting the dead," Wike said forcefully, as if trying to get it through the others' skulls. "We're being hunted."

"So you reckon' there ain't never been no dead for us to find?" Robert asked.

"That's what I am trying to tell you," Wike said. "Don't know who or what, but something's out here. Something that's playing with us like a cat plays with a mouse. It knows these lands. Has to be pretty darn fast, too. It must've killed Mathew's group in the night and then came for us. Didn't have time enough left to make its move before dawn so it got ahead of us and left Matt's head as a warning. Now whether it's saying we're dead next or just to stay the heck off its trail, I don't know, but our best bet of staying alive is to get back home. Something tells me, it won't follow us into town."

Wike's gaze fell on Robert as he asked what must have been one of the dumbest questions Wike ever heard. "How do you know it's not just the dead?"

"Son," Wike said slowly, "the dead don't show off their kills. They eat them. Mathew's head wasn't gnawed on and discarded; it was cut off and mounted for show."

"Zek's still out there with the party he took north." Alan sat up in his saddle. "They will be waiting on us at the Byrne's farm tonight."

"If they ain't dead, too," Ed spat. "I'm with Wike. We head back to town right now. Don't like being a target for something I can't see."

Louis shook his head. "We have to give Zek the benefit of the doubt. He might be alive and need our help."

"Zek can handle himself," Wike said.

"Would've said the same thing about Mathew an hour ago," Louis added. "Whatever is going on, there's strength to be found in numbers. The Byrnes' farm is a heck of a lot closer than town. We need to give Zek a chance to make it back and then we'll ride in together."

"Zek and them must be on their way by now," Robert said. "Have to be if they're planning on making it before the sun sets."

"Looks like you get the deciding vote, Alan. You with Wike and Ed, or us?" Louis asked.

"I don't know the first thing about crap like this. I shouldn't even be out here," Alan snapped.

"Nonetheless, it's on you now. Either way, sitting out in the open like this is a bad idea. Make the call so we can get moving."

"The farm, then," Alan said.

"The farm it is," Wike said. "At least there, there'll be cover."

6

THE SUN WAS already dropping behind the mountains as the group reached their destination. It was as barren and still as when they'd left it the day before. There was no sign of Zek's group or any survivors who might have escaped whatever happened to Mathew. Alan knew they all felt it, though nothing was said. Something had followed them from the sands and lurked somewhere just beyond sight, waiting for nightfall.

No one wanted to dismount and head into the house at the center of the farm. It was large with a small second floor. In the growing shadows, anything could be inside waiting for them. Yet the house *did* offer protection. Once it was secured, it could easily be defended.

Ed, Robert, and Louis took the horses to tie them up and do a sweep of the barn, leaving Wike and Alan to search through the house. Alan knew his rifle would be useless in such close quarters so he slung it onto his shoulder and drew his Glock, readying it. Wike left his own gun in its holster, opting instead to yank the massive knife Alan had once seen him sharpening from its sheath.

"After you," Alan said.

Wike smiled. "You're learning. That's a good thing."

They moved cautiously onto the front porch. Wike tested the door and found it unlocked. The two of them entered. The living room was cluttered with toys, liquor bottles, soiled plates, and signs it had seen a lot of use right up until the last moments of the Byrnes' lives.

"Take the upstairs," Wike told Alan. "I'll handle this

part of the house. We'll wait on the rest to take a peek in the cellar."

The steps creaked as Alan worked his way through the mess the Byrne family apparently had lived in. He tried to remember just how many kids John Byrne had fathered. The upstairs consisted of a single open room that contained four small beds, two dressers, and one tall mirror that sat in the right-hand corner of the room. The smell of blood and death lingered on the air, but there was nothing more threatening than dirty bed sheets and a little girl's dolls.

Alan descended the stairs to see Ed, Louis, and Robert coming in the front door.

"Clear upstairs," he told them.

Wike poked his head around the corner of the door that led to the kitchen. "Good. Ed, Robert, go straight back to the horses and get the cannon. Help Alan set it up at the window on the second floor. Should give us a nice edge." Wike's voice dripped with a malicious-sounding zeal. "When that's done, Louis, you're with me. The rest of the house is clear, too, so I don't see any point in risking checking out the cellar. If there's dead things down there, I would rather just seal them in than deal with them now. We have bigger problems at the moment. We'll seal it off and board up the back door, too. Anyone coming in will have to use the front where we'll be waiting."

The pounding of hammers echoed downstairs as Ed helped Alan assemble the portable tripod he'd brought for the cannon and got it situated at the room's sole window, facing the house's front yard. Alan clicked the ammo belt into the huge gun's feeder and then sat on one of the small beds. He was tired and the day was taking its toll on him.

"Looks like you could use some coffee," Ed said. "Suppose we all could at that."

Alan grinned. "You offering to make some?"

"Getting mighty dark." Ed took a peek around the cannon at the yard below. "Hope they're about done down there. Might not be long until we have company."

A few minutes later, Wike popped into the upstairs room. "Alan, I heard some of your old world stuff can let a man see in the dark. You got anything like that with you?"

Alan picked up his rifle from where it sat by the bed. "Yeah. I got a night scope right here."

"I need you to use it. You're going to be our eyes up here. You see anything, you either start shooting or yell down to us, understood?"

Alan nodded.

"I'll have Robert bring you up some coffee. Got a pot on in the kitchen. Didn't see no point in suffering on without it while we are waiting on Zek or whatever comes tonight. Might as well be comfortable, right?" Wike started back down then stopped. "Come on, Ed. We're gonna need all the rest of us on the first floor. There's a dang, blessed bunch of windows to cover."

Alan took a mini-tool kit from his pants pocket and removed the scope from his rifle. He moved to the window and held it like a looking glass, taking in the scene outside. The lowlight scope worked beautifully, amplifying the starlight to a level equal to that of the rays of a midday sun. In the distance, dark clouds gathered and a storm looked to be rolling in. His gaze drifted to the grounds of the house once more and noticed the man crouching beside the barn. He must have been invisible to the others in the darkness. Alan refocused the scope to get as good of a look at the intruder as he could. The man wore tattered clothing, presumably from age and wear. His skin appeared tough and leathery, scarred from exposure to the elements. An unnatural tick ran through his body every few seconds, causing his head to twitch slightly. Alan noticed he carried no rifle and didn't appear to have a gun belt. Instead, clutched in his quivering hands, was a bow, notched and ready. A serrated, metal arrow sat in the bow's string as if waiting to taste blood. The edges of its razored tip glinted in the starlight ever so slightly. Alan didn't believe for a moment the man was alone either.

No matter how good a killer the man might be, Alan doubted he could have taken Mathew's entire party on his own. There had to be others. Where were they? He swept the scope around, craning his neck to take in as much of the surrounding area as he could.

His breath caught when he saw them. There were indeed others—dozens of them. They were hidden in the shadows where those below his position wouldn't be able to see them. They were everywhere now. Some crawled on their stomachs like animals towards the house, while others scaled the sides of the barn. The crawlers carried swords and knives, either in their hands or clutched between their teeth. The ones on the barn wore bows strapped to their backs.

Alan weighed his options. He could open fire, but at which ones? Wiping out the crawlers would be an easy task for the cannon, but it would leave the climbers free to reach the barn's roof and return fire. Likewise, if he went for those on the roof, there was nothing to stop the dozens on the ground from leaping to their feet and charging the house in numbers so great that Wike and the others might get overwhelmed. Each hesitated second made things worse. Yelling down as Wike had instructed him was out of the question. It would tip off the shadow men outside they were aware of their presence as surely as if he opened up with the cannon.

Finally, he made a choice. Saying a prayer under his breath, he gripped the cannon and leaned its multi-barreled tip at the men slowly advancing towards the house. Its barrels whirred as they came to life . . . and the thunder started. Each barrel discharged as the cannon spun to life and spat a stream of unending lead into the men below. Alan took them completely off guard and they had no defense against the cannon's deadly blaze. Their bodies turned to pulp and sprays of blood as the cannon's shower of death tore them to shreds. The men's screams were like nothing he had heard before. They sounded more animal than human as they howled in the throes of death. He heard Wike and the others open fire from downstairs as well, though he couldn't guess what they were shooting at. It wasn't at the men scaling the barn. They remained undetected, and just as he had feared, reached positions where they could take their own shots at the house. A wave of arrows flew through the night. Some thudded in the wall near the window he fired from. One arrow streaked through the window, narrowly missed him and thunked home into one of the beds behind. Glass shattered downstairs and someone screamed.

He swung the barrel of the cannon up and over to take aim at the bowmen on the barn as the second wave of attackers came on strong. They poured down from the hills and raced across the fields towards the house, too spread out from him to make easy targets of them. Rifles cracked and six guns boomed below his feet as more glass shattered and the sounds of people struggling in close combat drifted up to him. Alan's arch of fire cut a strip through the barn's wood, killing several of the bowmen in the process. A second wave of arrows whistled their way to the house. He crouched down and took cover. The attacker's aim had improved. He ducked down even further as an arrow clattered off the cannon in front him and nearly sliced into one of his hands. He hit the floor hard as others flew over him and landed in the wall above. He hauled himself back up on his knees and made for the stairs. It was too dangerous to use the cannon now. The shooters knew exactly where to fire and a single shot could end his time on Earth.

His Glock held in a white-knuckled grip, Alan reached the edge of the stairs.

Ed lay there, sprawled forward, obviously having tried to make his way up before he fell. Three metal arrow shafts stuck out of his back, his shirt sopping wet with blood. Ed's breathing was ragged and labored. Alan guessed at least one of the arrows must have punctured a lung. Ed eyes met his own; Alan saw his fear, the kind of terror every man felt when he knew his time has come. Ed opened his mouth to try and say something; blood gushed from it onto the wooden step against his head. His eyes closed, he didn't move.

The sound of gunfire had fallen quiet, but Alan heard a struggle coming from the living room. He crept halfway down the stairs and peered through the guardrail. Wike wrestled with two of the men from the yard. Wike thrust his large knife into the taller of the two. The blade slid into the man's stomach. Wike gave it a twist and wrenched it free. The man's entrails spilled onto the floor. With a backhand slash to the man's neck, Wike ended him. The man's body toppled to the floor, blood spraying from the wound.

The other attacker slammed a crudely-made hatchet into Wike's back with a wet thud. Wike grunted from the pain. The tracker spun and rammed his knife up through the man's lower jaw. Alan could have sworn he saw its tip stick out of the top of the man's head for a brief second before he fell from view, taking Wike's blade with him.

"Wike!" Alan yelled, moving a bit further down the stairs.

The tracker turned to him, but as he did an arrow struck his side and caused Wike to drop to his knees.

"Run!" Wike yelled as three more men burst into the house via the room's broken main windows.

Alan leapt to his feet and sprinted towards them, firing his Glock. His first trio of shots nailed the closest of the three in the chest and sent him toppling over backwards. His fourth shot, slightly more aimed, hit the second in the forehead, snapping his neck back. The third man gave a bloodcurdling howl and threw himself at him. Alan fired, emptying the rest of his clip. Enough of the shots struck home to send the man to Hades and careening out of Alan's path.

Alan popped out his empty clip and shoved a fresh one into his Glock. He slipped on the blood that covered the floor as he entered the kitchen, narrowly avoiding ending up on his back from the fall. He caught himself by the door frame and flung himself onward, his momentum continuing. God was with him. No more of the men had entered the house yet. He could hear them outside giving shouts and yells in a mangled version of English that sounded both savage and primitive.

Alan noticed the cellar door and knew it was his only chance. He couldn't fight his way through all of the men outside. Crashing into the door, he cursed as his shoulder smashed into the heavy wood. Somehow the cabinets the others had moved to seal it off were already shoved aside. He wondered if maybe Robert or Louis had the same idea he did and just didn't live long enough to make it down. He ripped the door open and almost fell down the basement's steps to the darkness below. He went through the door and slammed it shut behind him. He threw the massive locking bar into place and crouched on the stairs. All he could do now was wait and pray the men hadn't seen him enter and wouldn't bother to check the house thoroughly for survivors. He kept his Glock aimed at the door with a pair of trembling hands. Minutes passed like hours. He heard the men enter the house, jumping around, giving victory shouts and beating their chests and the walls. He heard things dragged across the floor above and the wet sounds of meat hacked at by blades. Finally, there was the clinking of glass as the men exited back out the windows and, he hoped, vanished into the night.

1

ALAN HAD NO idea how long he sat on the steps before he found the courage to move again. When he was as sure as he could be the attackers were gone, he removed the bar from the door and stepped out of the basement. The weak rays of the morning sun came through the broken windows and stung his eyes. He took a moment and let himself adjust to the light. With his Glock ready, he ventured through the house. He counted the bodies of eight of the attackers scattered throughout then did a double take. Bodies? Sweat beaded on his skin as he stood in place and watched the closest one. Why hadn't it gotten up already? It should be roaming around and trying to find someone to eat right now not lying face down on the floor in a pool of blood. Then he noticed the bodies of his friends were gone, but even that didn't make sense. He could tell from the trail of congealed blood and the scuffing of the floor they had been dragged outside. The savages must have made sure his friends were truly dead then carried their corpses into the sands with them. Just as shocking, however, was that some of the attackers that lay dead were women.

Alan summoned up his courage, betting the dead couldn't play possum worth a crap, and bent over the body of a woman he placed in her mid-twenties, and examined her. He prodded her with the barrel of his Glock to be sure she was truly dead, then studied her closely. Her body stank of body odor and fecal matter. The clothes she wore were a mix of tattered green pieces of cloth and animal skins. Ritualistic scars covered her from head to toe as if someone repeatedly slashed her with a knife at intervals as she aged. A necklace of teeth and bones hung from her neck. Alan wasn't schooled in medicine, but he could tell even in his ignorance of such things that she was diseased somehow. Still, he reached and opened her mouth to get a better look at her teeth. They were in terrible shape and each one was filed to a point. The pain from doing such a thing must have been close to unbearable.

"Who in Hades are these people?" Alan said. A quick and careful inspection of the others in the house revealed the same. All of them were unkempt, sick, scarred, and possessed the filed teeth like the woman. None of them gave so much as a moan or sign of stirring from their deaths, and none had head wounds to keep them from doing so. The larger males—there were two of them—didn't wear the bone necklaces, however. Instead, they wore chains around their necks that held flat metal tags. Alan went cold inside as he recognized what they were. He reached under his own shirt and pulled out the tags that once belonged to his great grandfather. These savages . . . these monsters were "military."

Alan slumped against the living room wall as that realization slammed home. He refused to believe it.

Getting to his feet, he rushed outside. There were fifteen more bodies in the yard, most mangled and pulped from the cannon. All of them were the same as the ones inside and again the larger males wore the tags around their necks. What did it mean? How could these brutes be something he'd been taught to respect and honor his whole life through the stories passed along his family line?

The reality of his situation forced him to put his questions aside. He was alone; the horses were, of course, gone, except for one that had been gutted and sliced up for meat. The savages could just be over the hill and could return at any time. With no horse, it was going to be a long walk to Hyattsburg and he could only carry so much with him. Heading home wasn't an option. Someone needed to get the word to folks that these monsters were out here. If they were bold enough or greater in number than what he'd seen last night, they might even make a run on the town. It would be a massacre if the town had no time to prepare.

Alan tried hard to remember how many creatures he'd seen during the battle. It all happened so fast, but he was sure the corpses he'd shockingly found accounted for less than half of their number. Their weapons were primitive, but that didn't matter. From what he could gather about them from the battle and the bodies, all of them, each one, was a warrior and likely raised to be a killer from the moment they were born. Again he wondered where they came from and why in all the years since Hyattsburg was founded why no one had encountered them before. At least so far as he was aware. Why did they surface now? Who were they? Had they brought the dead with them?

He felt no desire to bury the bodies of the savages. Anyone who ate the flesh of another man could no longer be considered such themselves. But there was no other reason he could think of for them to take their kills with them.

He refilled his canteen and a second one taken from the house at the Byrnes' well pump, gathered some stale biscuits from the kitchen—which he hoped were still edible—and collected his rifle from the room upstairs. It was bizarre they hadn't taken any of the dropped weapons his friends had carried. He wondered if they simply didn't understand what the weapons were or if it was a matter of honor among them to kill their prey with their own hands.

With his gear collected, he turned his back to the rising sun and walked towards Hyattsburg. It pained him to leave the cannon behind, but there was nothing for it. Even if he left all else, it was simply too much and too bulky to carry all the way to town alone. His pace quickened with each step. Alan wanted to leave the smell of death behind as quickly as possible. He made no effort to attempt to cover his tracks. If these folks could out fox Wike while leaving no signs of their own trail, they could surely find him if they wanted to regardless of any action he might take.

8

THE DAY PASSED; his feet grew sore and his muscles ached. He ate on the move, nibbling at the rock-like biscuits he carried. When at last night fell, the darkness forced him to stop as the storm that had stalked him in the distance finally overtook him. Rain fell in waves and lightning danced in the clouds above. He found a small rock face in a hillside and ducked under it. The wind blew the rain in anyway, but he hoped he was safe from the lightning.

Alan struggled to stay awake, trying to estimate how much ground he'd covered and how far he had left to go to town, but his exhaustion was too great. His body betrayed him and in spite of the rain, he was soon asleep.

He awoke sopping wet and chilled to the bone. The storm had passed and the sky was clear. The shallow darkness held the hint of a new day and told him it was just before dawn. He unscrewed a canteen and took a drink. His sore body resisted his efforts to stand, but he forced himself to his feet anyway, using the rocks to pull himself up with a grunt. A heavy sigh escaped his lips as he hefted his pack and rifle onto his shoulders and continued his journey. Nothing ever seemed to go easy for him.

The day passed and so did another night as he grew weaker and Hyattsburg grew closer. His rations were gone and his water ran low. What could've been covered on horseback in half a day had taken his out-of-shape and not-used-to-the-elements legs two.

Time passed, and finally he stood staring into the

valley of Hyattsburg. He saw none of the traffic he remembered. Usually there were several riders or even a wagon or two coming or going from the town at any given point during the day. He heard no sounds of people conducting business or chatting in the streets. There were only buildings and an empty road as he approached.

Alan reached the edge of town and came to a stop at Gretchen's dress shop, the most outlying building. He leaned against its wall, catching his breath, his heart racing from exhaustion and dread. A woman's scream rang out from somewhere up the street. Ever so carefully, he poked his head around the corner and glanced down the street.

A massive, savage man dressed in animal skins and green rags emerged from the general store dragging a young lady by her long black hair. Alan recognized her as being the store owner's, Mr. Pressely's, daughter. He couldn't remember her name, but he recalled her as being polite and friendly. Her dress was soiled and splotched with red. Her hands clawed at the man's hold on her to no avail. The brute merely delivered a whopping blow to her head with his fist and she went limp. Alan pulled back some as another of the savages came flying out of the store's front door, dancing happily onto the road. This smaller one was a teenager from the looks of him and he rushed about gleefully, playing as he waved a wrinkled hand—not his own—through the air. Alan supposed the hand once belonged to Mr. Pressely. He unconsciously raised his fingers to hold his lips shut as the boy took a bite from the wrinkled hand and ground up its flesh between his teeth. Alan tried to look away and found he couldn't as the man ignored the boy and lowered himself over Mr. Pressely's daughter, shoving up her dress and pushing her thighs apart. He gripped the butt of his

Glock in the holster on his belt. Where was everyone? Had the savages already finished everyone else in Hyattsburg? His body shook with rage and fear as he heard the man grunt while he slid between the woman's legs and pushed himself inside her. With a scream, the girl tried to wiggle out from under him, but the savage slapped her then punched her in the throat.

Alan's Glock was halfway out of its holster when the world erupted into chaos as a wagon came clanking down the road into town. An elderly lady held the reins; she whipped the horses, forcing them to move as fast as they could. Dr. West rode shotgun beside her, aiming a rifle as carefully as he could on the bouncing wagon. It cracked twice, and the second shot sent the man sprawling from Mr. Pressely's daughter. The fellow landed face up with a hole in his head that leaked hot blood. The younger savage took one glance at his dead partner. The rifle now aimed at him, he vanished back into the general store. The wagon came to a lurching halt in the middle of the road as old Doc West jumped to the ground and ran for the girl. Alan recognized the elderly lady in the driver's seat as the Doc's wife, Tam. She hoisted a double-barreled shotgun to cover Doc as he gathered up the young woman.

"Doc!" Alan shouted, but wished he hadn't.

Tam whirled on him, emptying both barrels. Only the partial cover of the dress shop and his reflexes saved his life as he flopped to the dirt beneath the exploding wood above him.

"Hold up! Hold up, Tam!" Doc shouted. "That's Stephen's boy!"

"Don't shoot!" Alan yelled, hopping back to his feet.

"Get the heck over here, boy!" Doc said, watching the street and store front warily, his rifle held ready. "We gotta get the heck out of here!"

Alan ran to the wagon and threw himself up into it beside where Doc had laid the girl. He opted not to unsling his own rifle, favoring the faster rate of fire of his Glock in case they were rushed. The doc slid onto the front of the wagon with his wife and she stirred the horses into a frenzied, frantic dash. They raced through the town and into the hills on the other side.

Doc West glanced over his shoulder at Alan. "What the devil were you doing in Hyattsburg, son? Them things overran it yesterday."

"I was coming to warn folks about those . . . people."

The Doc laughed. "A little late for that. Where's Zek and his gang. Last I heard they'd gone out to fetch you."

"They're dead," Alan said flatly. "All of them. I'm the only one who made it back."

"Now that's a crying shame. We sure could use them right about now."

Alan gestured at the girl. "She going to be okay?"

"I think so. We've all got a fight on our hands, though. Gonna be hard for any of us to stay alive in the long run, I think."

"Where are we heading?"

"Back to my place," Doc said. "I got a feeling it's the last safe place left."

9

THE WEST ESTATE was the largest in all of Hyattsburg and its surrounding farmsteads. The bulk of the land was occupied by irrigated gardens and the old doctor's "green houses." His home, however, while not the sprawling mansion of the Gorios or the Camerons, was no less impressive to Alan now than it had been when he visited as a child with his dad. The building resembled the descriptions Alan's grandfather had painted of a military bunker than a proper home. It was shaped like a rectangular pill box and its walls were made of steel. The few windows Alan saw as they rode up to it were covered over with thick iron bars. Its slanted roof glittered in the sun from the hundreds of mirror-like panels that covered every inch of its top. He helped Doc West get the young girl off the wagon so they could carry her to the house. Its front door opened. Heather and Kristen, the doctor's two daughters, rushed outside, each holding Winchesters, which he noticed instantly were the work of his father.

"Dad!" Kristen wailed.

"Help us get her in the house," Doc West instructed them as Tam drove the wagon on to the next door stable to secure the horses.

"Where is everyone, Dad?" Heather asked, clearly surprised to see her mother and father back so soon and with only two people with them.

"This is it," Doc said grimly. Heather and Kristen disappeared ahead of them into the house, clearing the path for them.

As soon as Alan stepped in he shot the Doc a startled look. "You have electricity!"

"A bit," he replied, then barked, "Let's put her over there."

Alan helped him deposit the girl onto a comfortable-looking chair with real pillows on it, then turned to the Doc.

The Doc must have noticed the question in his gaze because he said, "It's solar-powered, and extremely limited, right, girls?"

Heather moved towards the door and flicked a switch on the wall beside it. As the light on the ceiling went out, she said, "Sorry, Dad. I'll get some candles."

The black-haired girl began to stir as Tam joined them all inside and Doc West tugged the vault-like door closed.

"Come on, Alan," he said, "Tam and the girls can take care of her. You and I, we need to talk."

Alan followed the doctor to his study. Doc West took a seat at his desk, and lit up a cigar with a match. He motioned, offering Alan the seat across from him. "Bet folks in town wouldn't think I'm so crazy now . . . if they were alive," he said with a sad laugh. "I'm not worried about those freaks. They can't get in here. Once this house is sealed up like this, an army couldn't get in. The question is . . . what are we going to do about them? We can't stay in here forever as much as I would like to sometimes."

Alan had no answer.

"Did you and Zek figure out where they're coming from? Who they are? All I know is they're sick and they're as hungry as the dead are. We're food, and maybe breeding stock to them, nothing more." The Doc leaned over his desk so close Alan smelled the smoke on his breath. "You're educated, sharp too. I can tell. You take after your father. Surely you can at least tell me this: are the dead inside the wall?"

"No. At least we didn't run into any real walkers from outside the wall," Alan said firmly. "And in spite of all the killing that's going on, I don't think there's more than a few, if any, random walkers out there. The savages eat their prey, like you said, and for some reason, they don't come back as walkers when they die."

West looked as if he'd been slapped hard across the face. "That's impossible!"

"I'm surprised you haven't noticed it if you've fought them. They just stay dead."

It was West's turn to stay silent as he let Alan's words sink in.

"That's not all that's strange about them either," Alan added. Reaching into his pocket, he tossed two sets of tags he'd taken from the savages' dead onto the desk. "The big males wear military tags from the world before the Fall."

"What does it mean?"

"They could be from beyond the wall. They wouldn't have any problem just climbing over it. They're not stone cold dumb like the dead are."

Doc West shook his head. "No. The wall was supposed to have defenses that kept us safe."

"So the wall's real, then?" Alan asked, feeling stupid.

"Of course it is!" West snapped. His expression softened. "Sorry, Alan. I know none of us from Hyattsburg have traveled to it in decades or more, but history says it's there. Logic says it has to be there. We know the dead virus is very real and that's what it was built to keep us safe from."

"What do you mean by defenses?" Alan's interest was

completely ensnared by the idea. "No automated system I know of from my family's tales could possibly still be active after all this time."

"You're right, yet the stories in my family say the wall's defense will never fail us." Doc West leaned back and appeared to think for a moment. He snapped his fingers as the light of an epiphany surged over him, then his face turned grim. "Alan, what if the system *wasn't* automated?"

They stared across the desk at each other as the room seemed to grow cold and time seemed to slow.

Clearing his throat, Alan changed the subject. "So everyone in the whole town is dead except us?"

Doc shook his head. "I never said that. I wasn't there when they made their run on Hyattsburg. Everything I know, I heard from Doc Gorio. He showed up here last night, barely alive, with half a metal arrow inside him. He didn't live to see the sun come up. I buried him myself this morning after putting a round through his skull. Ugly business, but it had to be done." The Doc took a puff of his cigar. "He said those cannibals came out of nowhere and just ran into town like a pack of animals, killing folks as they went. Sounded like folks never had a chance. The way he told it, they left all the women and children that they could alive unlike what I heard they did out at the Byrne place as few days back. Dr. Gorio said those things rounded them up afterwards and marched them from the place like cattle. He claimed they thought he was dead or he'd never have made it here. Said he crawled to the town stables while they were collecting the women folk and found a horse so he could make it to me. He knew this house would still be standing."

Alan rubbed his jaw. "Those poor people."

West nodded. "Death would've been better for them.

I'll confess I was hoping when you and Zek rode in with your posse, we'd go after them, save those we could."

"What about the other farmsteads? The Camerons' place? You think any of them are left?"

"Don't know, but even if they were I doubt there would be enough of us to try even if everyone was willing to give it a go. Most wouldn't be. My guess is there's at least fifty of those savages left breathing and maybe a lot more waiting out there in the sands."

"We can't just sit here and do nothing," Alan said. "Eventually, they'll run out of food or face whatever brought them here to begin with again and come back. We can't spend the rest of our lives living behind these walls in fear."

"I'm not disagreeing with you, but what can we do? I'm old, Alan, and while you may be one of the best weaponers Hyattsburg has ever seen, you're not a warrior. You're not even a lawman like Zek was and you said they killed him."

"I saw your daughters hefting rifles that my father made as we came in. I know you don't want to hear it, but we need everybody we got, Doc."

"Heather's tough like her mom and she can handle a weapon. Kristen wouldn't last five seconds out there, though."

"Do you have any other weapons here?"

"We have those two rifles plus my own, a shotgun, and two pistols. One six shooter your father made for me and a .357 I won off him in a card game when you were just a wee lad. Only got twelve rounds for the Magnum and not many shells for the shotgun either. Always figured the rifles would be enough. This house is a fortress, remember?"

"Weapons aren't an issue if we can make it to my place," Alan said.

"I know." The doc laughed. "So, we're really going to do this? You're honestly going to sit there and ask me to risk my daughter's life so we can have a third gun with us after I saved your butt in town."

"It was your idea, Doc. I am just telling you what's going to have to be if we want to stand any sort of chance at all."

"I'll ask Heather. I am not forcing her into this."

Alan nodded. "I understand."

10

LATER, ALAN SAT in the living room with Heather, Kristen, and the black-haired young lady whose name he discovered was Mary. They all stared at the floor trying to pretend they couldn't hear the holy, raging argument from the kitchen between Doc and Tam. Heather and Mary both agreed to go with them. Alan didn't know if Mary would be of much use, but even a badly-aimed gun pointed in the right direction would be a help at this point. He winced as he heard something shatter and Tam's voice climbed higher in volume. The old lady didn't want her daughter to fall into the hands of the savages as food or worse. She didn't even want the Doc himself heading out with Alan, but the Doc was determined to make her see reason.

Finally, West emerged from the kitchen, looking tired but victorious. "Let's go now before she changes her mind." Alan, Heather, and Mary leaped to their feet and followed him outside to the stable. "Her and Kristen will be fine while we're gone as long as they keep the house sealed up," he said to no one in particular. Alan wondered if he was saying it to reassure himself.

As they readied the horses, the Doc added, "We'll hit your place first, Alan, get us some real firepower, and then we'll head up to the Camerons and see if anyone is left alive in that massive mansion of theirs."

Alan was in the lead as they rode out. Heather and Mary followed him closely, with Doc West bringing up the rear. Alan trusted the old man to keep an eye out for anything creeping up on them from behind. The ride to his own estate was a short one, taking less than two hours. His house was just like he left it. There was no sign the savages had come anywhere near the place. Still, he'd seen them fool Wike before so he kept his guard up as he brought his horse to a stop at the front door and tied it to the porch's railing. The others did the same.

"Ain't nothing in the house worth fooling with," Alan said. "What we need is out back in the work shed. Heather, you and Mary stay here. If you see anyone that ain't me or your dad, you shoot first and ask questions later. We'll be back in a few."

When they got to the work shed, Doc laughed that Alan had called the building a shed. It was large, the size of a normal person's house or larger. Alan fished a set of keys from his pocket and went to taking down the three locks that barred their way.

"Hate to hassle you, son, but aren't we in a hurry?" Doc said.

"Trust me," Alan replied, "you do not want to try to force this door."

"Boom?"

He nodded. "A big one. Dad taught me to live like he did and he always took great care to make sure our work never got into the wrong hands."

"Your dad was as tough as he was smart."

"Thank you." Alan glanced over at West as he finished with the last lock. He gently pushed the door inward. They entered the shed together. The Doc seemed to look at the walls covered floor to ceiling with weapons. He was clearly impressed by what he saw. There were boxes upon boxes of all types of ammunition and more guns than could easily be counted. Not all of them were the new kind Alan and his father had made a fact which Alan was proud of. Many were old world weapons which he had kept and taken great care of. A P-90 lay on a table and looked as if it had been in the process of being cleaned but abandoned for something more important. A real M-16 and an AR 15 hung displayed on one wall and across the room hung a .30.06 and many other hunting rifles where they too were displayed.

"I think we'll need some shock and awe," Alan said. "Rate of fire will be more important to us than dead-on accuracy given how badly they'll likely outnumber us." He selected the best of the old world stuff he had and gathered it into a pile containing three UZIs, a M-16 rifle, his dad's cherished AK-47, and three Glock 17Cs counting the one he carried with him.

"Are those real, working, fully-automatic UZIs?"

"Yep. All of these are in as good of shape as the day they were made. Mom used to say my dad loved these weapons more than he did her . . . when she was mad at him." Alan walked over to a chest in the rear left corner of the work room and flipped up its lid. Inside was a suit of old world combat armor. He put it on as Doc continued to look around. Alan holstered two of the UZIs onto his waist, strapped two of the Glocks into holsters on his thighs, and picked up a backpack that he crammed full with every clip he owned. Finally, he picked up the AK-47 and turned to see the Doc appraising one of his father's swords and swinging it through the air. Its blade was handcrafted and razor-sharp.

"Didn't know your dad made blades, too," the Doc said, looking ashamed at taking the sword without asking.

Alan reached over and took it from him. "He made weapons in all their forms. He was an artisan of death."

"Wouldn't hurt to take some of them with us, too."

Alan shrugged. "You're right. Better safe than sorry." He added a scabbard to his back and took the sword from the Doc's hands. He slid the sword into the scabbard.

Heather was given the remaining UZI, the last Glock, and a sleek knife made for combat. Doc took the M-16 and held onto his magnum for his sidearm. The old man refused to take a blade of his own, saying if the savages got close enough for him to need one, he'd be dead anyway. They left Mary with a Winchester because out of all of them she needed the weapon's accuracy. She was far from being a good shot and the rifle would not only give her a better chance of hitting her intended target, but also force her to think about each shot as she fired it. They equipped her with a gun belt holding a six shooter as well. Alan even wore a pair of infrared goggles pushed up onto his head above his eyes. It would give them the edge he hoped for, if they ran into combat at night. He only wished he had more of them to pass on to the others, but there was only the single pair in his supply. In his backpack, he also carried what was possibly the last amount of C-4 in the entire world. His father had truly been a genius, and at last all of his work and the things he'd spent his life watching over were about to be put to use doing some real good. Alan hoped it would be enough.

The next order of business was to see if they could rustle up any help. They needed every gun hand they could get and it was Alan's hope there was someone left alive up at the Camerons' mansion. The Cameron place was back and out of the main routes of travel; he hoped the savages had passed it by without ever knowing it was there. It very well might be a waste of time to try because the Camerons could all be dead, but if there was even a single man left in the family it was worth the chance. Every person they had increased the odds they would survive when they caught up to the party of savages. Yes, the cannibals had a good lead on them already and gained ground every minute Alan wasted, but they had horses and the savages didn't. He figured they could overtake them even if they made the stop at the mansion, so it was worth the gamble.

II

THE CAMERON ESTATE'S perimeter was surrounded by a fence, a living barricade composed of tall spines of cactus known as Ocotillo. It was a cheap and easily maintained fence that served its purpose just as well, if not better, than a manmade one. Alan and the Doc knew there was only one opening in the barricade and it rested on the side of the estate that faced Hyattsburg.

God was with them thus far, Alan felt. They hadn't run into a single savage. Talk about good news and bad news at the same time. While it kept them safe for the moment, it would make their pursuit of the cannibals complete guess work when the time came.

The group found the opening in the Ocotillo fence and headed onto the estate proper. They rode slowly, keeping a watchful eye for any trouble that might be waiting on them. Alan noticed Heather kept stealing glances at him. A continuous smirk stayed on her lips as she did.

He slowed his pace and let her overtake him so they rode side-by-side. "What is it?" he asked.

"What?" she said, plainly feigning innocence.

"You know what I mean. Why do you keep smirking like that? We may all be riding to our deaths."

"You look ridiculous," she said. "What in the devil are you wearing?"

Alan cheeks flushed red. "It . . . it's a combat suit. The old world military's special operatives always wore these into battle."

Heather stared at him. His embarrassment forced him to

think he needed to explain more. "It's made from stuff that can stop bullets," he said, trying to sound strong and proud.

"The savages don't use bullets," she sharply pointed out.

"I know that." he snapped.

"Then why are you still wearing it?"

Alan bit his tongue, holding his growing anger in check. "It felt right to wear it, okay? My great grandfather wore it when he served his tour of duty and helped build the wall. Besides, if it can stop bullets, it can stop arrows. Make sense?"

"Okay, fine." Heather smiled a real, full-on smile. "All you had to do was say so."

Not knowing how to respond, he kicked his horse's sides and pulled ahead of her. He'd never understood women like he had guns and he reckoned he never would.

As they approached the mansion in the center of the Cameron grounds, Doc rode up to join him.

"Alan," Doc said.

The weaponer saw what had drawn the Doc's attention: the shaft of a metal arrow protruding from the wood of the front door. Alan motioned for the others to stay in their saddles as he hopped to the ground. He moved closer to the house, climbing the steps leading to the porch. Blood seeped from beneath the cracked front door. Alan drew his right Glock and slowly pushed it open. He counted three dead savages lying in the huge foyer.

He heard the creature before he saw it.

The walker lunged at him from the left doorway leading into the living room. It wore the fine suit of a business man and Alan knew at once it was one of the Camerons. Its moan was loud and hungry. Numerous patches of its flesh were missing as if they had been cut from it in strips. Alan bet the savages had a go at the man's body before they decided to depart. There was also a hole in its left cheek that looked like a vicious bite wound. The body of one of the savages appeared to be gnawed on. Alan couldn't help but wonder if the walker and the savage had tried to eat the other. Somehow the corpse had gotten the upper hand. That much was obvious.

Out of instinct, Alan jerked up his pistol and fired off a three-round burst. The bullets thudded into the creature's chest, spraying blood, but did nothing to slow its attack. The dead thing closed in on him, grabbing his arms with its cold hands. The two of them fell back through the main door together, landing on the porch as they continued their struggle. The thing's teeth snapped at his face as he did his best to keep it shoved away from him.

"Get its head up!" Alan heard Doc yell. He would've been more than happy to oblige the doctor, but it was taking everything he had just to avoid getting his skin ripped away by the thing's yellow teeth. Its hunger drove it with a fury he could barely match. They rolled into the porch's railing and Alan found himself wedged between it and the monster. Its breath was foul and nauseating. Pain shot through him from the awkward angle his body was twisted up against the rail. It felt as if his spine was about to be snapped in two from the pressure. The monster seized his second of weakness and pushed forward. It would have taken a chunk from his shoulder except for the fact an UZI barrel slid between them. The UZI chattered, pulping the dead man's face at such pointblank range. Alan flinched as its lukewarm blood splattered over him. He shuddered and kicked its remains off of him, wiping his cheeks with his hands in an attempt to clean off the blood as fast as he could. He whirled to see Heather looking at him through the rails.

"Thank you," he croaked, and pulled himself to his feet. He turned to the front door half expecting another creature to come racing out of it. He retrieved his Glock from where he dropped it in the struggle and reentered the house. The others followed him this time and he welcomed their company.

The Doc glanced at the bodies of the savages. "Somebody sure put up a fight."

"The Camerons were a big family," Heather said. "How come Eli is the only one we've seen so far, if they're all dead?"

"Who's Eli?" Alan asked.

"The guy I just shot off you," she replied.

Alan blinked and glanced back out the door at the body on the porch.

"The savages could have taken the others, but I don't think so. It's more likely they are still here in the house somewhere, wandering aimlessly like Eli probably was until Alan disturbed him," the Doc said.

"I say we get the heck out of here now," Heather said. "Odds are we're not going to find any help here."

"Oh, but you would be wrong," a voice called from the stairs leading to the second floor of the mansion. A tall, gray-haired woman wearing a silk robe and holding a glass of wine effeminately waved at them. Alan saw the Doc roll his eyes at the sight of her.

"Hello, Kelly," Doc said, an edge in his voice.

"My good Doctor West, it has been a while since I have seen you, hasn't it?"

"Not long enough."

Kelly reached the bottom of the stairs and approached Alan. "And who might you be, young man?"

"Alan."

Kelly extended her hand to him as if she wanted him to take it in his own and kiss it. "Welcome to the Casa de Cameron."

Alan didn't take her hand. Instead, he nodded and said, "Thank you. Are you alone here?"

Kelly sipped at her wine. "Alas, I fear so. I don't think any of the boys made it through the battle. It's truly a shame."

There was something wrong with this woman, but Alan didn't know if she was merely drunk or completely delusional and in shock from the horrors she endured this morning. She acted as if everything was suddenly normal again, which was far from the truth. He hoped the doc had a plan.

"Kelly." The doc snapped his fingers in an effort to make the woman focus.. "What happened here? Are there more of the dead around?"

Her smile crumbled from her lips as her eyes grew tight with anger. She walked to the closest corpse and kicked it. "These . . . these animals murdered my family!"

Alan kept his mouth shut and followed Doc's lead.

The Doc drew closer to her and she threw herself into his arms, sobbing. "Oh, Michael, they came this morning. We didn't even know they were here until Charles was already dead. He was headed out to feed the horses like he does every day. He opened the door and there was one of them, a big man with sickly yellow eyes. His knife slashed Charles' throat open so fast we barely saw him move. Harold and Mark ran to get their guns and Eli . . . little Eli charged the man to keep him away from me. Eli tackled him and they crashed into the wall. I heard Eli scream. He let go of the man and turned to me. I'll never forget the look on his face. There was a hole in his chest where that animal had shoved his knife inside him and twisted it around. Harold and Mark came racing back into the foyer and they let the animal have it. Their rifles were so loud, like a shower of thunder, it hurt my ears. The next thing I knew, Harold was yelling for me to get upstairs. The big man was dead, but there were four more like him trying to get inside. I ran. It's what Harold told me to do. The boys always knew what was best when it came to things like that. I had to listen to him. I went upstairs to my bedroom, locked the door, and stayed there. In a few minutes, the gunfire and the screaming were over with. I hid in my closest for a long time, waiting on the boys to come and tell me everything was okay, but they never did. Luckily, I had a bottle of spirits from my evening drink I had forgotten to put away in my bedroom. I took some to calm my nerves. By the time I poured my second glass, I could hear someone banging around down here again. I stayed in my room and watched the yard from my bedroom window. When I saw you riding up, I decided it was time to come down." Then, almost as if in afterthought, "Besides, I had to give you a proper welcome. We get so few visitors out here."

As she finished, the Doc pull back from her embrace. "She's got a fever, Alan," he said as he wiped his hands on his jacket. The Doc's expression told him something was very wrong. To Kelly,

"There's something you're not telling us."

She grimaced, her face so taut it was a wonder she even got the words out.

"I'm hurting, can't you see that? My family was just murdered and you can't even be civil enough to comfort me without calling me a liar! Get out. All of you. Take your guns and leave."

Alan saw it as she threw her arms in the air. Beneath

the sleeve of her robe, on her right arm, was clearly a bite mark.

"Shoot her, Alan," the Doc said, regret in his voice.

Alan stared at him as Kelly yelled, "How dare you? This is my house! How dare you accuse me of being infected!"

There was a rifle, likely used by her sons during the battle, lying at the base of the stairs. She went for it. Alan moved to intercept her before she reached it, but the Doc was faster. He drew his .357 and fired. The shot blew off half of Kelly's head and sent her to the floor.

Alan went for Doc's gun, but the doctor shoved him back.

"I don't know how or when, but she must've come downstairs before we got here and found Eli herself. Somehow he got a bite out of her. It was just a matter of time until she became a walker too, and you know it," Doc said.

"Dad's right," Heather said. "You could see the sheen of sweat on her skin if you looked hard enough. She had the virus."

Alan stood over Kelly's body, feeling sorry for her. Hadn't there been enough death already?

"It's not safe here and there's no help to be found." The Doc was already halfway to the door. "If the rest of the Camerons actually managed to fight off the savages into a retreat somehow and died of their own wounds, there could be more walkers. It's time to go."

Alan found a quilt in the living room and covered Kelly's corpse before he followed the others outside. The group saddled up.

"Where are we going now?" Mark squeaked, apparently shaken from what he'd witnessed in the house.

"To collect our vengeance," Alan said coldly, kicking his horse into motion. He rode west without looking back.

12

ALAN WANTED TO push through the night, but the Doc and Mary were on the verge of falling off their horses and couldn't go on. Heather appeared haggard as well, but Alan could tell she was handling the physical stress of the day better than the others. He stopped the company with a raise of his hand. They were well beyond the limits of Hyattsburg now and there was no remotely secure cover to be found. The best the desert offered was a hill with an outcropping of rock. At least camping next to it, they'd only have three directions to watch not four. The rock was formed so the only path for the savages to come at them was if they scaled its face on the other side of the hill and dropped onto them from above. It was a tactic so fraught with risk, Alan believed even the savages would think twice before attempting it.

Whether or not to permit a fire was a hot topic of debate among the group. Alan didn't want one because he figured it would draw the savages like flies, but Doc and Heather insisted they were likely long gone and it would be safe to do so. It was a certainty that their main pack was as they tended to stay on the move. Outnumbered, but not completely convinced, Alan relented and helped Heather gather what they could for fuel as the Doc plopped onto his butt, leaned against the rock face, and almost instantly started snoring. Alan couldn't blame him. Doc was up in years and the day they'd had was far from an easy one. Mary sat beside the old man with her Winchester across her lap, appearing frightened and regretful of joining them on this journey.

Soon, Alan had the fire going. He sat beside it and warmed his hands. The temperature fell quickly with the sun gone from the sky. Heather took a seat next to him after checking to make sure her father was comfortable and well.

Alan picked up a twig and poked at the flames, sending glowing embers drifting into the darkness around them.

"It's hard to believe, isn't it?" Heather asked quietly.

"What?"

"How much our lives have changed so fast?"

"I remember when my dad died. I thought the world had come to an end that day."

"I'm sorry," she said, and he knew she meant it.

"I can't imagine what the people who were alive before the Fall felt like when the dead first started to rise. I knew my dad would become a walker and attack me if I didn't . . ." He paused. "Can you imagine your father, mother, or best friend getting up hungry without knowing it was coming? It's a miracle there're any of us left alive."

"Close to a thousand souls, gone in a matter of days." Heather held back her tears; Alan could sense her resolve to stay strong. "Those savages had no reason to come after us. We could have helped them if they were starving or sick. All they had to do was ask. Because of them, our race may really be dead now. We were so few before compared to the billions of the old world. For all we know, we're it, Alan. Everything we did, everything we are, may be lost thanks to them."

Alan shrugged. "It's not over yet. If we save the folks they took, we can start over again. Build things back to the way they were." He turned toward her. Heather's grief over a dying planet was evident. "Don't surrender hope. You lose it and the fight is already over. They'll have won and that'll be the end of it."

A weak smile stretched over her lips. "Tell me everything will be okay."

"I can't do that," he said. "Not honestly. But I can tell you we'll do our best to make it that way." He took a deep breath and exhaled slowly. "You should get some rest. I'll keep watch."

"No," Mary said, joining them at the fire. "You need rest too, Alan. We all need you as sharp as you can be. You're our weapon, gunsmith." She sighed. "I'm too scared to sleep, anyway. I'll keep watch."

"Yes, ma'am." Alan moved closer to Doc and spread out his bedroll on the dirt. He laid down and noticed Heather standing over him.

"Can I join you?" she asked.

Alan felt his skin go hot and knew he must be a beaming shade of red. She must have noticed because she quickly said, "Not like that. I just want to be held. I don't think I can take being alone tonight."

He scooted over and she laid down beside him. He pulled her close. She put a hand on his arm and closed her eyes. Alan hoped she would sleep well because he sure wasn't going to with her warm body pressed against his.

But sleep eventually came, comfy, peaceful.

When he awoke, Heather sat at the fire attempting to cobble together a passable breakfast from their meager stash of supplies. Mary lay on the ground, her head resting on the Doc's rolled-up coat, dead to the world. Doc tended to the horses and made sure they were ready for the day ahead.

Alan sat up, feeling uncomfortable about his closeness with Heather the night before. He wondered if the Doc knew and how the old man felt about it. There was no time to corner him and find out, however. After a quick breakfast of jerky, coffee, and things that once were supposed to have been biscuits, the group was on the move.

It wasn't long until they saw the wall in the distance and Alan knew all the stories about it being out here were just as real as the dead themselves. It stretched across the horizon to the east and west as far as he could see. The wall was a testament to the wonders the old world could create even with its civilization collapsing and teetering on the edge of death.

He took a pair of binoculars from the porch to get a better look at what lay ahead.

Below the wall appeared to be a camp. He adjusted his focus. Not a camp; it was a full-on village. There was a massive building-like structure that protruded from the wall itself and looked to be a part of it. Around the bunker stood a sea of weathered and time-worn tents and other shelters that seemed to be made by more primitive means. They resembled the tee-pees once used by Native Americans his father had shown him pictures of in their small collection of history books.

The whole area was a flurry of activity. Savages waded through the ranks of prisoners taken in Hyattsburg, who appeared to have only recently arrived. Alan watched as one savage with wild, matted hair and a face half-covered with scars, grabbed a woman and forced her mouth open. The savage probed her teeth with his filthy fingers. Some kind of sorting was clearly taking place as the savages inspected the newcomers.

Alan handed his binoculars over to Doc. "I counted around a hundred and fifty of them, including their children. Lord only knows how many more of them are in that building and the tents."

"I reckon you need to come up with a plan, then."

The Doc laughed. "Riding in there guns blazing is only going to get us and those poor folks from town killed."

"We should find some cover," Heather said. "They likely have scouts guarding their perimeter just like we would. We don't want to be seen. Surprise is about the only thing we have going for us at the moment."

Alan nodded, taking back the binoculars.

The small group sought cover in the dunes to wait for nightfall and form a plan. It was decided they would try to slip into the villages under the cover of darkness. Their hope wasn't to win a victory against the savages, but merely to rescue those they'd taken. From what Alan and the Doc could tell, none of the prisoners had been bound. They just needed some courage and a distraction to make a run for it. Alan had all the distraction they needed tucked in his backpack in the form of C-4. If it thinned the savages' numbers in the process, that was merely a bonus. Heather and Mary could rally the folks from Hyattsburg and get them ready to move while he and the Doc set the explosives to cover their escape.

13

BY THE GRACE of God, they made it through the day without being discovered. The horses were secured and left behind as they crept towards the camp. Doc carried a portion of the C-4 and a detonator with him, taking the direct route into the camp. Heather and Mary came in from the east while Alan approached from the west.

Alan reached the edge of the encampment well ahead of the others thanks to the advantage his infra-goggles gave him. A savage stood guard at the perimeter. Alan wound his way through the dunes to get as close to the man as he could before he made his move. It wasn't close enough to take the guard down without risking him alerting the others. He pounced from the shadows, drawing his sword, and charged the savage. The savage's eyes bugged out as he saw Alan coming for him. He opened his mouth to scream, but Alan's blade took his head from his shoulders with a single, desperate slash.

The camp remained quiet and Alan slumped to his knees, saying a prayer of thanks before he continued into the camp. The savages' security was greatly lacking. He wondered if they'd ever been attacked at the wall before and was inclined to doubt it. Their guards were lazy and apathetic in his estimate of things. The camp stunk of disease, filth, and cooked human flesh. He carefully moved through the tents to the bunker. Almost everyone seemed to be asleep. He resisted the urge to kill the sleeping savages he passed. Doing so would accomplish nothing in the greater scheme of things and would put the entire plan at risk.

He was within a dozen feet of the bunker's wall when he heard chaos erupt on the other side of the camp where the bulk of people from Hyattsburg were. So much for stealth, he thought as a hulking male savage sat up in front of him. The man snarled, showing wolf-like teeth, and reached for the hatchet beside him on the ground. Alan grabbed an UZI from the holster on his hip and fired at the man pointblank. The savage fell back to the dirt, bleeding and gasping from a dozen holes in his chest.

Alan whirled around to see three more running at him, two women waving curved blades and another man wielding something akin to a battle ax. He emptied the remainder of his UZI's clip and sent the creatures to Hell in a blaze of fully-automatic fire. Seven more took their place, closing in on him from every direction. He ran for the bunker and slapped his entire pack of C-4 onto its wall then darted deeper into the camp. His hands were a blur as he drew his matching Glocks and shot the savages that sprang into his path. His legs pumped beneath him as a burly, little man covered in thick black hair from head to toe stepped in front of him, thrusting a spear at his stomach. Alan dodged the spear's tip by sidestepping it, and put a round into the man's forehead. The savage's body spun. Alan shoved him aside and kept running.

Hyattsburg folk and savages alike screamed from terror and panic. He heard the chatter of an M-16 up ahead. He sped up, trying to reach the area where it was coming from, but an explosion lit up the night and the outer wave of its blast knocked him from his feet. A woman was on him before he had the chance to get up. Drool from her pieced and swollen lips leaked onto his cheek as she growled and snapped at him with her filed teeth. He managed to position one of his Glocks under her chin and squeezed the trigger. Sticky drops of blood splattered onto him as the bullet ripped its way through the top of her skull. He rolled her corpse from him and emptied the last few rounds in his other Glock into a rail-thin teenager in a loincloth that came at him with a knife held high above his head.

Frag it, Alan thought as he tore the detonator for the C-4 from his pocket and triggered the explosives. The ground shook as half of the bunker became shrapnel and flying debris behind him. The savages around him hit the dirt. The fear on their faces was clear. Alan made use of it and sprinted passed them. People ran from the camp on all sides now, savages and Hyattsburg folk alike. He knew there was nothing more he could do. Either the prisoners would get free or they wouldn't. All he had time to think about was making it out of the camp alive. Alan chose the path with the least number of savages between him and the desert. He bolted, discarding his empty Glocks as he ran. He had no use for them, not without any more ammo. He drew his UZI.

Alan cut a swathe of death before him. Three of the cannibals rushed to meet him as he ran forward; their bodies shook and danced as stream of automatic fire hit them head on. Even as they fell, more took their place. Again his UZI blazed, catching the first savage in his stomach and turning its guts to a bloody, pulpy mess that oozed onto the sand as the man toppled over and lay still. Alan jerked the UZI up, aiming for the face of a woman with filed-down, razor-like teeth who came at him with a knife in her hand. He emptied the remainder of his clip into her until the gun clicked empty. Tossing his Uzi aside, he yanked his sword free from its scabbard once more. He dispatched two more of the savages that moved to block his escape, gutting one and slicing a second's nose from his face with a wild, panicked slash. Finally, he was through their lines.

As he broke free of the camp, a new sound arose from the battlefield that caused him to freeze in place and turn to stare back at the remains of the bunker. Through its shattered walls, the dead poured onto the sand. Alan's heart sunk as he realized the bunker or some inner part of it must've connected directly to the world beyond the wall. In blowing half of the bunker to bits, he'd breached the wall for the dead. He stood watching the remaining savages near the creatures forget about their fleeing prisoners and turn to engage the dead whose moans and growls were rang on the air. Alan almost started back to help them, but knew it was hopeless. There looked to be no end to the stream of dead running out from the hole in the bunker. Half of the few savages left had already fallen to their cold, grasping hands and gnawing teeth.

Alan did the only thing he could and vanished into darkness of the desert night like a ghost.

19

WHEN HE STOPPED for the night and settled in to wait for the dawn, he did so without dinner or a fire. He was too tired to attempt a fire and knew it would only bring unwanted company anyway. Alan stretched out on the sand and slept with his goggles on and his sword within easy reach. All his other weapons were lost except for the special one he still held in the pocket of his combat suit. The grenade brought him no comfort, however. It was not a weapon that would help him in the close combat he was bound to face if the dead or the savages came calling. His heart broke as he wondered about the others. Had Heather escaped? He knew there was nothing he could do but pray as exhaustion claimed him.

He awoke a few hours later to find a savage sitting on his haunches a few feet away, staring at him. The man was into his forties from the looks of him, and was well toned with the thickness of muscle that had spent its life fighting to survive in a culture where the weak were served for lunch.

"You. . ." The man gestured at Alan. "You are the death bringer. All dead now. Rotting ones will eat us together, your people and mine."

Alan reached for his sword to discover it gone. He kept his calm and asked, "What do you want?"

"To live." The man grunted. "See your magic fire. You destroy pen where dead let in. Think you have more. It keep us alive longer."

"Pen?" Alan said. "You let the dead in through that bunker and kept them there?"

"Had to eat. Not enough of us. Let dead in, few at a time. Eat them but begin to make us sick. Kept them for food. No other source."

"That's why you came to Hyattsburg? You needed fresh meat because eating the dead was making your people sick?"

"Yes." The man stood up. "We go. Dead coming. Smell them."

Alan listened; snarls rose in the distance.

The savage tossed him his sword. "Must go or die."

He disliked this animal-like creature that looked like a man, with whom he was now stuck with but saw little choice for an alternative. He needed all the help he could get. If the savage made a move against him, he'd settle things then. For now, they had to work together if they both wanted to stay alive. Alan vowed to himself to keep an eye on the cannibal as they ran through the dunes side-by-side. The savage readied his bow, notching a metal arrow on its string, as a dead woman dressed in a soiled petticoat and nothing else leaped from the top of a dune into their path. The savage loosed his arrow, slaying the walker as the arrow entered its head through the left eye, without slowing. She toppled to the sand and lay there twitching.

"More come!" the savage yelled. "Must move faster!"

Alan struggled to keep pace. "We have to get back to my town. It's the only chance we have."

"This way." The savage changed his direction. Alan followed him in silence. The sounds of snarls fell behind them; the dead must've lost their scent.

When the savage stopped, Alan did so as well. The savage smiled at him with brownish, pointed teeth. "You give me magic fire, I leave you breathing."

"Are we headed towards my town?"

The savage lifted his arm and pointed ahead. "It lies there."

Alan didn't wait for the savage to speak again. His sword whipped through the air. Its blade embedded itself in the side of the savage's head. Alan yanked the blade free as the man collapsed onto the sand. He wiped the blade clean on the man's animal skin vest and sheathed the blade.

He traveled on in the way the savage had shown him until he reached the Doc's estate. He didn't even get close enough to the Doc's house to see it. He could hear the dead, all worked up into a frenzy around the house, trying to get inside. Alan steered wide of the house and headed for his own. If he was going to die, he wanted it to be there.

15

HE STUMBLED ONTO his porch as the sky grew dark with gathering rain clouds. Alan locked his door behind him and plopped himself down in the kitchen. He sat at his table for some time before his emotions caught up with him. Tears slid over his cheeks and he broke into open, loud sobs. He'd failed in all he'd set out to do and watched helplessly as his friends and everyone he knew died around him. He lowered his head onto his arms and wept until the sound of falling rain pulled him from his pain. Alan thought about the Doc, Heather, and those who must have surely died at the savages' camp. Life wasn't fair. None of them deserved such a fate, especially not Heather. She was young, beautiful and strong. Alan knew deep inside that she was stronger than he was. He doubted very much she would be sitting here sobbing now. Cry though she may, Heather wouldn't give up. She'd be doing something to help those who remained.

Alan stood up and wiped his red eyes. He knew the dead would be coming tonight. This time, he *would* be ready for them, waiting to send as many of the monsters back to Hell as he could. If he was able to thin their ranks, even at the cost of his own life, those left alive at Doc's place and others, would have a much brighter chance at surviving the terror that was coming.

He walked to his work shed and began his preparations as the rain grew heavier and the darkness fully closed in. He had plenty of surprises up his sleeve for the dead, including some left behind by his father.

THE WEAPONER

That night, Alan sat staring out between the cracks in the boards he'd nailed over the kitchen window. He turned the crank of the alarm system his father installed years before. He thanked God it still worked. Its sirens wailed into the rain. He hoped it would not only draw the dead who would've stumbled upon his house anyway, but all of them in Hyattsburg as well. Even as the first creatures came into view on the horizon, he kept turning the crank. While his home was nowhere near the armored fortress the Doc's was, his father had built it to be easily defended. All of the windows on the first floor other than the boarded-up one in the kitchen were far too small for a human to squeeze through. The walls of the house were made of thick reinforced wood as were the front and back doors. Eventually they would give, but not for a while.

Alan let go of the crank and headed upstairs. He reached the bedroom window as the fastest of the dead came bounding into his yard. He smiled, and rolled the Gatling gun that he'd hauled up from his work shed closer to it so its barrel struck through the window. He spun up the gun. It didn't have the firepower or the rate of fire of the massive old world weapon he'd been forced to abandon at the Byrnes', but it would do the job.

Its barrels spat a shower of lead as they whirled. He moved it side-to–side, sweeping over the ranks of the dead as they ran towards the house. One man so rotted his body barely held together lost an arm then took two more rounds in the chest before completely falling apart as he went down. Another creature had its knee shattered by a round of lead then went splashing through the mud, tumbling over itself as rain continued to pour from the clouds above. A naked man took a series of rounds that cut into him across his waist and nearly tore him in half. His insides spilled into his hands and he stopped to stare at them in wonder. Still another dead man took a very unlucky hit to the head and left this world to return to wherever it came.

Alan kept the Gatling roaring even as some of the dead made it past his field of fire and reached the house's first floor. He heard them slamming themselves again and again into the house's barred front door. The Gatling's fire quickly muted the sound. Ears ringing something fierce, he figured the attack on the house downstairs was far worse than it sounded to his aching ears. The old-fashioned weapon had done its job, however. He left it smoking, grabbing up a rifle, and half-ran-half-jumped down the stairs to the first floor. The front door still held firm. It shook violently in its frame but refused to yield to the dead's pounding fists. Alan took a quick moment and shoved his couch up against it in an effort to reinforce the barrier then raced into the kitchen.

A swarm of groping hands reached through the barely-holding boards on the window. It grew weaker with each passing second and a good third of Alan's reinforcements to it had already been torn apart. The back door held up well though. It sounded as if most of the things were still on the front side of the house. He emptied the Winchester into the things clawing at the window through the holes in the boards. He tossed the rifle aside and turned to the kitchen table. On it rested five six shooters, another rifle, and two double-barreled shotguns, all prepped and ready. As the last of the boards over the window fell away, he grabbed up the closest shotgun and fired. Its barrels boomed like thunder, echoing in the room even over the howls of the hungry dead. The dead man trying to crawl through became an exploding mess of stale blood and pulp. Not bothering to waste time he didn't have reloading, he discarded the shotgun and snatched up the other one, emptying it into the dead as well.

He stood his ground by the table and watched, waiting, as several creatures managed to crawl inside and tumble onto the kitchen floor. He waited until the things were on their feet, then cocked the two six shooters and dispatched each of them with quick but carefully-aimed shots to their heads. He repeated the process of death until the kitchen floor was cluttered with unmoving corpses and he had only one six shooter left. He tucked it into his belt, picking up his last rifle, and backed away from the table as the dead gained ground. Every few steps he took in retreat, Alan stopped and sent another of the creatures to Hell with a crack of his Winchester.

With a loud *crack*, the front door caved inwards and the dead burst in, an entire horde of them. Alan counted a dozen already inside and hundreds more waited outside, trying to shove their way in. He swung himself onto the stairs and fled. The dead's footfalls thudded on the steps behind him as they gave chase.

He darted into his bedroom and slammed the door. He spun the Gatling around to face the entrance and didn't even wait for the door to be forced open. He cranked the weapon as fast as he could, spinning its barrels, and tearing the dead to shreds as they started to come through. This time, between the Gatling's rate of fire and the narrow entrance to the bedroom, he was able to hold them at bay. The gun's belt of bullets got shorter and shorter. The gun was so hot it burned his skin, but he kept it going until its belt fully ran out.

As the dead flooded the room over the bodies of

their fallen brethren, Alan gave up his position and flung himself through the bedroom window, hoping to buy more time. He caught edge of the roof and pulled himself onto the top of the house. The roof was slick from the rain and his fingers slipped. For a terrifying moment that seemed an eternity, he thought he would fall to his death into the waiting mass of the dead below. His hands shot out, grabbing for the roof's edge—anything—that would save him. Barely catching the edge, he swung his body into the side of the house with a heavy thud. He grunted from the pain and strained to heave himself upwards. He swung his right leg up onto the roof, then rolled the rest of himself onto it. Rain pelted his face as he looked up at the dark sky above and he muttered a quick prayer of thanks. He was alive, and through sheer force of will had bought himself a bit more time before the dead caught up with him.

Alan hurried to the highest part of the roof and looked down at the army of the dead all around the house. They were everywhere, pressed dozens deep against the walls. The ones at the front were getting crushed from the weight of those behind as the horde continued to shove forward more determined than ever when they saw him on the roof. Alan estimated their number to be in the hundreds. All he had left was the last six shooter tucked in his belt. He drew it and smiled. His plan had worked as well as he could've hoped for and then some. The noise of the alarm sirens and the Gatlin gun's thunder had drawn the dead to him like flies.

Then he saw them. At the top of the hill, on the trail leading to his home, there was a group of riders. He could tell even from this distance they were all women. Somehow Heather or Mary, perhaps both of them, must have survived the battle at the savages' camp. They must have heard his sirens and were on their way to try to rescue him. Their effort was futile, suicidal, and some might claim flat-out stupid, but it touched his heart and gave him hope. Maybe his plan to go out in a blaze of glory would actually do some good. At least temporarily, what he was about to do would greatly reduce the number of dead those left alive would have to deal with until more made their way in from the breach in the wall. Maybe if nothing else, he would be giving them a greater chance at continued survival.

Two dead men climbed onto the roof with him and crawled towards him. Alan pulled the detonator his dad had designed from his pocket with one hand and dispatched the closer of the two creatures with a head shot from his pistol with the other, splattering the creature's brains onto the wind.

"Time for us to go," he said as he felt the other dead man's frigid, wet hand close around his ankle. He flipped the detonator's cover open with his thumb and then pushed its trigger. The explosives his father had lined the walls of the house with and stored in its dirt basement erupted as he screamed and the flames washed over him.

16

TEN MINUTES EARLIER, Heather pushed her horse hard approaching Alan's home as he fought his last battle, its hooves splashing water and slinging mud as it ran. Mary and the three other women that escaped the savages rode with her to save Alan. Each of them were as armed as they could be from the limited supply of weapons and ammo left at the Doc's. Heather had seen her father die today. He'd stood tall and proud, his M-16 blazing away in his wrinkled hands, slaughtering the savages that wanted to taste his flesh. He'd seen her and Mary, too. She remembered how he'd looked at them with sadness and determination to see they stayed alive as he set off the C-4 he had with him. His death saved their lives and quite likely Alan's as well. Somehow the Weaponer had made it home only to be trapped in what appeared to be a fatal struggle with the dead. At first the sound of thundering fire from some sort of heavy weapon was heard before they even came into view of the house. When it ceased, there was still the chatter of small arms fire. There were too many of the dead surrounding the house to even attempt to count. There moans and snarls rose above the noise of the battle but now the sound of gunfire had fallen silent within the house. She prayed they weren't too late.

Almost all of the dead that made it inside the wall were gathered at the house, but there were a few stragglers still roaming about. Every so often one of them would notice her party and come tearing at them, growling, a hungry gleam in its eyes. A man who she recognized as the saloon owner, Pete, did so now. Without slowing her horse, Heather leveled her rifle at him and blasted him from the trail. The shot struck him in his shoulder and its impact spun him out of her way as she galloped passed.

None of the women saw the explosion coming. It just happened. Alan's house lit the night with flames so intense Heather felt the heat even at her distance. Her horse bucked and attempted to bolt, but she forced it to stand steady, holding tightly to its reigns. The others managed to stay in their saddles, too, except for Mary. Her horse threw her from its saddle and she landed hard on the ground with the sickening, snapping sound of breaking bone. Her body lay bent at an angle; she writhed in pain. Heather's mind reeled, trying to take in all that was happening. A wave of secondary explosions rocked the night as Alan and his dad's workshop and ammo depots went up, toasting even more of the dead. Heather knew in her heart Alan was gone. There was no way anyone could have survived the explosion that turned his house into a mass of flames and flying shrapnel. She forced herself to focus on Mary and those who had followed her here.

Mary looked up at her with blood seeping from her mouth as she spoke. "My back's broken. Please . . . please don't let me become one of those monsters."

Right thing to do or not, Heather felt like a monster herself as she led her horse to Mary and pressed the barrel of her Winchester to the skin of her friend's forehead.

"I'm sorry," Heather whispered as she squeezed the trigger.

One of the other women, Anna, a fiery redhead with a temper to match, yelled at her. "Watch out!"

Heather glanced over her shoulder to see what appeared to be a dead twelve-year-old boy shambling towards her. One of the boy's legs was broken with the off-white of bone showing through his decayed flesh. She spun around, bringing up her rifle, and fired a single shot that shattered his other leg and sent him sprawling face first into the mud. Heather took a final look at the remains of Alan's burning home then motioned for the others to follow her. They tore off into the night.

Her mother, sister, and the handful of other survivors were waiting on them to return.

EPILOGUE

TWO DAYS LATER, Heather was so tired she just wanted to drop onto the floor and never move again. The rain poured down outside. All of the rivers were up and many of the low lying areas were flooded. Water filled the streets of Hyattsburg, reaching a grown man's thighs at its deepest. Still, she always returned from her supply run covered in blood, sweat, and mud. The rain never washed it all away. Today's trip was the last. She wouldn't be heading out again for a very long time if she *ever* did again. Anna, herself, and the others who were able had looted and gathered almost everything they could find that would help them stay alive. The water helped keep the dead at bay, but that wouldn't last forever. Soon, the creatures would be so thick outside that making it to town would be impossible. Alan's sacrifice had bought them time and nothing more. It had greatly reduced the number of the dead they'd had to deal with at one time, but with the wall breached, more and more of the creatures poured inside its boundaries every day. They were safe, though, as long as they stayed inside. Her father's house was virtually impenetrable to the point that even an armed and organized force would have trouble getting in. For the mindless dead, it was impossible. There were eighteen survivors counting herself: her mom, her sister, five other women, three young girls, and seven boys all under the age of ten. Between her father's stockpiles and what they had gathered from town, she estimated they had enough food to feed them for close to four months if it was rationed properly. Water wasn't an issue. There were well pumps inside the house and even a few working pieces of old world plumbing that could be run when the solar cells on the roof had filled their batteries to the peak.

The main problems were ammo and the tight quarters; they had no choice but to share. Their ammo supply consisted of maybe two hundred rounds total for their rifles, less than half that for the pistols, and less than a dozen remaining shotgun shells. If the dead ever did get inside, their last stand would be a short one. And while the house was large compared to most in Hyattsburg and its surrounding farmsteads, it simply wasn't built to house so many souls for a prolonged period.

Tensions and depression ran high and were their greatest enemies. Often tempers flared and Heather became the sheriff of the house, breaking up fist fights and moderating disputes. The weight of the world found a new home: her shoulders, as she was the strongest and most cunning of those still breathing. She missed her father and Alan terribly, but there was no choice but to hold it together and carry on. The others depended on her to stay strong and lead them through this nightmare, and she swore she'd keep them all breathing for as long as she could.

About the Author

Eric S. Brown is a zombie author living in North Carolina. He has been called "the king of zombies" by places like Dread Central, and was featured in the books *Zombie CSU: The Forensics of the Living Dead*, *Wanted Undead or Alive*, and *Halloween Nation: The Secrets of America's Fright Night* as an expert on the genre.

His novel, *The War of the Worlds Plus Blood, Guts and Zombies*, has just been released from Simon and Schuster. Some of his other books include *Bigfoot War*, *Unabridged Unabashed and Undead: The Best of Eric S Brown*, *Barren Earth*, *Season of Rot*, *World War of the Dead*, *Zombies II: Inhuman*, *Season of Death*, and *The Human Experiment* to name only a few.

His short fiction has been published hundreds of times in the small press and beyond. Some of his anthology appearances include *Dead Worlds I, II, III*, and *V*, *The Blackest Death I* and *II*, *The Undead I* and *II*, *Dead History*, *Dead Science*, *Zombology I* and *II*, *The Zombist*, *War of the Worlds: Frontlines*, and many others. He also writes an ongoing column on the world of comic books for *Abandoned Towers* magazine and a column about his own experiences as a writer for *Morpheus Tales Magazine*.

He is currently at work on *Bigfoot War II*.

COSCOM
ENTERTAINMENT
Where Imagination is Truth

www.coscomentertainment.com

Lightning Source UK Ltd.
Milton Keynes UK
UKOW051955240213

206754UK00001B/3/P